Fallen Too Far

Also by

ABBI GLINES

THE SEABREEZE SERIES

Breathe

Because of Low

While it Lasts

Just for Now

Never Too Far

The Vincent Boys

The Vincent Brothers

Fallen Too Far

Abbi Glines

SIMON AND SCHUSTER

First published in Great Britain in 2013 by Simon and Schuster UK Ltd
A CBS COMPANY

1 3 5 7 9 10 8 6 4 2

Simon & Schuster UK Ltd
1st Floor, 222 Gray's Inn Road
London
WC1X 8HB

Simon & Schuster Australia, Sydney

Simon & Schuster India, New Delhi

A CIP catalogue record for this book is available from the British Library.

PB ISBN 978-1-4711-3467-8
eBook ISBN 978-1-4711-1860-9

Printed and bound by CPI Group (UK) Ltd, Croydon, CR0 4YY

www.simonandschuster.co.uk
www.simonandschuster.com.au

Abbi loves to hear from her readers. You can connect with her on
Facebook: Abbi Glines (Official Author Page)
Twitter: @abbiglines
Website: www.abbiglines.com

To Liz Reinhardt who was my own personal cheerleader while I wrote this book. You come across people in life that become one of those friends you can't imagine life without. Liz is one of those friends.

ABOUT THE AUTHOR

Abbi Glines can be found hanging out with rock stars, taking out her yacht on weekends for a party cruise, sky diving, or surfing in Maui. Okay maybe she needs to keep her imagination focused on her writing only. In the real world, Abbi can be found hauling kids (several who seem to show up that don't belong to her) to all their social events, hiding under the covers with her MacBook in hopes her husband won't catch her watching Buffy on Netflix again, and sneaking off to Barnes and Noble to spend hours lost in the yummy goodness of books. If you want to find her then check Twitter first, because she has a severe addiction to tweeting @abbiglines. She also blogs regularly but rarely about anything life changing. She also really enjoys talking about herself in third person. www.abbiglines.com

Rush and Blaire's steamy summer continues in...

ONE

Trucks with mud on the tires were what I was used to seeing parked outside a house party. Expensive foreign cars weren't. This place had at least twenty of them covering up the long driveway. I pulled my mom's fifteen- year-old Ford truck over onto the sandy grass so that I wouldn't be blocking anyone in. Dad hadn't told me that he was having a party tonight. He hadn't told me much of anything.

He also hadn't shown up for my mother's funeral. If I didn't need somewhere to live, I wouldn't be here. I'd had to sell the small house that my grandmother had left us to pay off the last of mom's medical bills. All I had left were my clothes and the truck. Calling my father, after he had failed to come even once during the three years my mother had fought cancer, had been hard. It had been necessary though; he was the only family I had left.

I stared at the massive three-story house that sat directly on the white sand in Rosemary Beach, Florida. This was my dad's new home. His new family. I wasn't going to fit in here.

My truck door was suddenly jerked open. On instinct, I reached under the seat and grabbed my nine-millimeter. I swung it up and directly at the intruder, holding it with both hands ready to pull back on the trigger.

"Whoa . . . I was gonna tell you that you were lost but I'll tell you whatever the hell you want me to as long as you put that thing away." A guy with brown shaggy hair tucked behind his ears stood on the other side of my gun with both his hands in the air and eyes wide.

I cocked an eyebrow and held my gun steady. I still didn't know who this guy was. Jerking someone's truck door open wasn't a normal greeting for a stranger. "No, I don't think I'm lost. Is this Abraham Wynn's house?"

The guy swallowed nervously, "Uh, I can't think with that pointed in my face. You're making me very nervous, sweetheart. Could you put it down before you have an accident?"

Accident? Really? This guy was beginning to piss me off. "I don't know you. It's dark outside and I'm in a strange place, alone. So, forgive me if I don't feel very safe at the moment. You can trust me when I tell you that there won't be an accident. I can handle a gun. Very well."

The guy didn't appear to believe me and now that I was looking at him he didn't appear to be real threatening. Nevertheless, I wasn't ready to lower my gun just yet.

"Abraham?" he repeated slowly and started to shake his head then stopped, "Wait, Abe is Rush's new stepdad. I met him before he and Georgianna left for Paris."

Paris? Rush? What? I waited for more of an explanation but the guy continued to stare at the gun and hold his breath. Keeping my eyes on him, I lowered my protection and made sure to put the safety back on before tucking it under my seat. Maybe with the gun put away the guy could focus and explain.

"Do you even have a license for that thing?" he asked incredulously.

I wasn't in the mood to talk about my right to bear arms. I needed answers.

"Abraham is in Paris?" I asked, needing confirmation. He knew I was coming today. We'd talked just last week after I'd sold the house.

The guy nodded slowly and his stance relaxed. "You know him?"

Not really. I had seen him twice since he'd walked out on my mom and me five years ago. I remembered the Dad who'd come to my soccer games and grilled burgers outside for the neighborhood block parties. The Dad I'd had until the day my twin sister Valerie was killed in a car accident. My father had been driving. He'd changed that day. The man that didn't call me and make sure I was okay while I took care of my sick mother, I didn't know him. Not at all.

"I'm his daughter, Blaire."

The guy's eyes went wide and he threw back his head and laughed. Why was this funny? I waited for him to explain when he held out his hand. "Come on Blaire, I have someone you need to meet. He's gonna love this."

I stared down at his hand and reached for my purse.

"Are you packing in your purse too? Should I warn everyone not to piss you off?" The teasing lilt to his voice kept me from saying something rude.

"You opened my door without knocking. I was scared."

"Your instant reaction to being scared is to pull out a gun on someone? Damn girl, where are you from? Most girls I know squeal or some shit like that."

Most girls he knew hadn't been forced to protect themselves for the past three years. I'd had my mother to take care of but no one to take care of me. "I'm from Alabama," I replied, ignoring his hand and stepping out of the truck myself.

The sea breeze hit my face and the salty smell of the beach was unmistakable. I'd never seen the beach before. At least not in person. I'd seen pictures and movies. But the smell, it was exactly like I expected it to be.

"So it's true what they say about girls from Bama," he replied and I turned my attention to him.

"What do you mean?"

His eyes scanned down my body and back up to my face. A grin stretched slowly across his face. "Tight jeans, tank tops, and a gun. Damn, I've been living in the wrong fucking state."

Rolling my eyes, I reached into the back of the truck. I had a suitcase and then several boxes that I needed to drop off at the Goodwill.

"Here, let me get it." He stepped around me then reached into the truck bed for the large piece of luggage my mom had kept tucked away in her closet for that "road trip" we never got to take. She always talked about how we'd drive across the country and then up the west coast one day. Then she'd gotten sick.

Shaking off the memories, I focused on the present. "Thank you, uh . . . I don't think I got your name."

The guy pulled the suitcase out then turned back to me.

"What? You forgot to ask when you had the nine-millimeter pointed at my face?" he replied.

I sighed. Okay, maybe I'd gone a little overboard with the gun but he'd scared me.

"I'm Grant, a, uh, friend of Rush's."

"Rush?" There was that name again. Who was Rush?

Grant's grin grew big once again. "You don't know who Rush is?" He was extremely amused. "I'm so fucking glad I came tonight."

He nodded his head toward the house, "Come on. I'll introduce you."

I walked beside him as he led me to the house. The music inside got louder as we got closer. If my dad wasn't here, then who was? I knew Georgianna was his new wife but that was all I knew. Was this a party her kids were having? How old were they? She did have kids, didn't she? I couldn't remember. Dad had been vague. He'd said I'd like my new family but he hadn't said who that family was exactly.

"So, does Rush live here?" I asked.

"Yeah, he does, at least in the summer. He moves to his other houses according to the season."

"His other houses?"

Grant chuckled, "You don't know anything about this family your dad has married into, do you, Blaire?"

He had no idea. I shook my head.

"Quick mini lesson then before we walk inside the madness," he replied, stopping at the top of the stairs leading to the front door and looked at me. "Rush Finlay is your stepbrother. He's the only child of the famous drummer for Slacker Demon, Dean Finlay. His parents never married. His mother, Georgianna, was a groupie back in the day. This is his house. His mother gets to live here because he allows it." He stopped and looked back at the door, as it swung open. "These are all his friends."

A tall, willowy, strawberry blonde wearing a short royal blue dress and a pair of heels that I'd break my neck in if I tried to wear them stood there staring at me. I didn't miss the distaste in her scowl. I didn't know much about people like this but I did know that my department store clothing wasn't something she approved of. Either that or I had a bug crawling on me.

"Well, hello Nannette," Grant replied, in an annoyed tone.

"Who is she?" the girl asked, shifting her gaze to Grant.

"A friend. Wipe the snarl off your face Nan, it isn't an attractive look for you," he replied, reaching over to grab my hand and pull me into the house behind him.

The room wasn't as full as I'd assumed. As we walked past the large open foyer an arched doorway led into what I assumed was a living room. Even so, it was bigger than my entire house or what had been my house. Two glass doors were standing open with a breathtaking view of the ocean. I wanted to see that up close.

"This way," Grant instructed as he made his way over to a . . . bar? Really? There was a bar in the house?

I glanced over the people we passed by. They all paused for a moment and gave me a quick once over. I stood out big time.

"Rush, meet Blaire, I believe she might belong to you. I found her outside looking a little lost," Grant said and I swung my gaze from the curious people to see who this Rush was.

Oh.

Oh. My.

"Is that so?" Rush replied in a lazy drawl and leaned forward from his relaxed position on the white sofa with a beer in his hand. "She's cute but she's young. Can't say she's mine."

"Oh, she's yours alright. Seeing as her daddy has run off to Paris with your momma for the next few weeks. I'd say this one now belongs to you. I'd gladly offer her a room at my place if you want. That is if she promises to leave her deadly weapon in the truck."

Rush narrowed his eyes and studied me closely. They were an odd color. Stunningly unusual. They weren't brown. They weren't hazel. They were a warm color with some silver laced through them. I'd never seen anything like them. Could they be contacts?

"That doesn't make her mine," he finally replied and leaned back on the sofa where he'd been reclining when we walked up.

Grant cleared his throat. "You're kidding, right?"

Rush didn't reply. Instead he took a drink from the longneck bottle in his hands. His gaze had shifted to Grant's and I could see the warning there. I was going to be asked to leave. This wasn't good. I had exactly twenty dollars in my purse and I was almost out of gas. I'd already sold anything of value that I possessed. When I'd called my father I had explained that I just needed somewhere to stay until I could get a job and make enough money to go find a place of my own. He had quickly agreed and given me this address telling me he would love for me to come stay with him.

Rush's attention was back on me. He was waiting on me to make a move. What did he expect me to say? A smirk touched his lips and he winked at me.

"I got a house full of guests tonight and my bed's already full." He shifted his eyes to Grant. "I think it's best if we let her go find a hotel until I can get in touch with her *daddy*."

The disgust on his tongue as he said the words "daddy" hadn't gone unnoticed. He didn't like my father. I couldn't blame him really. This wasn't his fault. My dad had sent me here. I'd wasted most of my money on gas and food driving here. Why had I trusted that man?

I reached over and grabbed the handle on the suitcase that Grant was still holding. "He's right. I should go. This was a very bad idea," I explained without looking at him. I tugged hard on the suitcase and he let go somewhat reluctantly. Tears stung my eyes as the realization that I was about to be homeless sunk in. I couldn't look at either of them.

Turning, I headed for the door, keeping my eyes downcast. I heard Grant arguing with Rush but I blocked it out. I didn't want to hear what that beautiful man said about me. He didn't like me. That much was obvious. My dad was not a welcome member of the family apparently.

"Leaving so soon?" a voice that reminded me of smooth syrup asked. I glanced up to see the delighted smile on the girl who had opened the door earlier. She hadn't wanted me here either. Was I that revolting to these people? I quickly dropped my eyes back to the floor and opened the door. I had too much pride for that mean bitch to see me cry.

Once I was safely outside I let out a sob and headed to my truck. If I hadn't been carrying my suitcase I'd have run. I needed the safety of it. I belonged inside my truck, not in this ridiculous house with these uppity people. I missed home. I missed my mom. Another sob broke free and I closed the door to my truck locking it behind me.

TWO

I wiped my eyes and forced myself to take a deep breath. I couldn't fall apart now. I hadn't fallen apart when I'd sat holding my mother's hand as she took her last breath. I hadn't fallen apart as they lowered her into the cold ground. And I hadn't fallen apart when I'd sold the only place I had to live. I would not fall apart now. I would get through this.

I didn't have enough money for a hotel room but I could live in my truck. Finding a safe place to park it at night would be my only problem. This town seemed safe enough but I was pretty sure this old truck parked anywhere overnight would draw attention. I'd have the cops knocking on my window before I could even fall asleep. I would have to use my last twenty dollars on fuel. Then I could drive into a larger city where my truck would go unnoticed in a parking lot.

Maybe I could park behind a restaurant and get a job there

too. I wouldn't need gas to get to and from work. My stomach growled reminding me that I hadn't eaten since this morning. I would need to spend a couple dollars on some food. Then pray I would find a job in the morning.

I would be okay. I turned my head to check behind me before I cranked the truck and backed out. Silver eyes stared back at me.

A small scream escaped me before I realized that it was Rush. What was he doing standing outside my truck? Had he come to make sure I left his property? I really didn't want to talk to him anymore. I started to turn my eyes away and focus on getting out of there when he cocked an eyebrow at me. What did that mean?

You know what? I really didn't care. Even if he looked ridiculously sexy doing it. I started to crank the truck but instead of the roar of the engine, I was met with a click and some silence. Oh no. Not now. Please not now.

I jiggled the key and prayed I was wrong. I knew the gas gauge was broken but I'd been watching the mileage. I shouldn't be out of gas. I had a few more miles. I know I did.

I slammed my palm against the steering wheel and called the truck a few choice names but nothing happened. I was stuck. Would Rush call the police? He wanted me off his property so badly he'd come out here to make sure I left. Now that I couldn't leave would he have me arrested? Or worse, call a tow truck. I did not have the money to get my truck back if he did that. At least in jail I'd have a bed and food.

Swallowing the lump lodged firmly in my throat I opened the truck door and hoped for the best.

"Problems?" he asked.

I wanted to scream at the top of my lungs in frustration. Instead, I managed a nod. "I'm out of gas." Rush let out a sigh. I didn't speak. I decided waiting on the verdict was the best option here. I could always beg and plead afterward.

"How old are you?"

What? Was he really asking me my age? I was stuck in his driveway, he wanted me to leave and instead of discussing my options, he was asking me my age. The guy was strange.

"Nineteen," I replied.

Rush raised both his eyebrows, "Really?"

I was trying hard not to get pissed off. I needed this guy to have mercy on me. Forcing the snide comment that was on the tip of my tongue back, I smiled. "Yes. Really."

Rush grinned and shrugged. "Sorry. You just look younger." He stopped and his eyes trailed down my body and back up again slowly. The sudden heat in my cheeks was embarrassing. "I take that back. Your body looks every bit of nineteen. It's that face of yours that looks so fresh and young. You don't wear makeup?"

Was that a question? What was he doing? I wanted to know what my immediate future held, not discuss the fact that wearing makeup was a luxury that I couldn't afford. Besides, Cain, my exboyfriend and current best friend, had always said I didn't need to add to my looks any. Whatever that meant.

"I'm out of gas. I have twenty dollars to my name. My *father* has run off and left me after telling me he'd help me get back on my feet. Trust me; he was the LAST person I wanted to ask for help. No, I don't wear makeup. I have bigger problems than looking pretty. Now, are you going to call the police or a tow truck? I prefer the police in case I get a choice." I snapped my mouth closed ending my rant. He'd pushed me too far and I hadn't been able to control my mouth. Now, I'd stupidly given him the stupid notion of a tow truck. Dangit.

Rush tilted his head and studied me. The silence was almost more than I could handle. I'd just shared a little too much information with this guy. He could make my life harder if he wanted to.

"I don't like your father and from the tone in your voice, neither do you," he said thoughtfully. "There is one room that is empty tonight. It will be until my mom gets home. I don't keep her maid around when she isn't here. Mrs. Henrietta only stops by to clean once a week while Mom is on vacation. You can have her bedroom under the stairs. It's small but it's got a bed."

He was offering me a room. I would not burst into tears. I could do that later tonight. I wasn't going to jail. Thank God.

"My only other option is this truck. I can assure you that what you're offering is much better. Thank you."

Rush frowned a moment, then it vanished quickly and he had an easy smile on his face again. "Where's your suitcase?" he asked.

I closed the truck door and walked over to the back of the truck to get it out. Before I could reach for it, a warm body that smelled foreign and delicious reached over me. I froze as Rush grabbed my luggage and pulled it out.

Turning around I looked up at him. He winked at me. "I can carry your bag. I'm not that big of an ass."

"Thank you, again," I stuttered, unable to look away from his gaze. Those eyes of his were incredible. The thick black lashes that framed them almost looked like eyeliner. He had an all-natural highlighter around his eyes. It was completely unfair. My lashes were blonde. What I wouldn't give for lashes like his.

"Ah, good, you stopped her. I was giving you five minutes and then coming out here to make sure you hadn't completely run her off." Grant's familiar voice snapped me out of my daze and I spun around thankful for an interruption. I had been gazing up at Rush like an idiot. I'm surprised he hadn't sent me packing again.

"She's gonna take Henrietta's room until I can get in touch with her father and figure something out." Rush sounded annoyed. He stepped around me and handed Grant the suitcase. "Here, you take her to her room. I have company to get back to."

Rush walked off without a backwards glance. It took all my willpower not to watch him walk away. Especially since his backside in a pair of jeans was extremely tempting. He was not someone I needed to be attracted to.

"He is one moody sonuvabitch," Grant said, shaking his head and looking back at me. I couldn't disagree with him.

"You don't have to carry my suitcase inside again," I said reaching for it.

Grant moved it back out of my reach. "I happen to be the charming brother. I'm not about to let you carry this suitcase when I have two very strong not to mention pretty damn impressive arms to carry them with."

I would have smiled if not for the one word that had just thrown me for a loop. "Brother?" I replied.

Grant smiled but the smile didn't reach his eyes. "I guess I forgot to mention that I'm the kid of Georgianna's husband number two. She stayed married to my dad from the time I was three years old and Rush was four until I was fifteen. By then, Rush and I were brothers. Just because my dad divorced his mom didn't change anything for us. We went to college together and even joined the same frat."

Oh. Okay. I hadn't been expecting that. "How many husbands has Georgianna had?"

Grant let out a short hard laugh then started walking toward the door. "Your dad is husband number four."

My dad was an idiot. This woman sounded like she went through husbands like she did panties. How long before she got rid of him and moved on?

Grant walked back up the steps and didn't say anything else to me while we headed toward the kitchen. It was massive with black marble countertops and elaborate appliances. It reminded me of something out of a home decorating magazine. Then he opened a door that looked like a large walk-in pantry. Confused, I looked around then followed him inside. He walked to the back of it and opened another door.

He had enough room to walk inside and put my suitcase on the bed. I followed him in and scooted around the twin size bed that left only a few inches between it and the door. It was obvious I was under the stairs. A small nightstand fit tightly between the bed and the wall. Other than that, there was nothing.

"I have no idea where you are supposed to keep your luggage. This room is small. I've never actually been back here." Grant shook his head and then sighed. "Listen, if you want to come to my apartment with me you can. I'll at least give you a bedroom that you can move around in."

As nice as Grant was I wasn't about to take him up on that offer. He didn't need an unwanted houseguest taking up one of his bedrooms. At least here I was tucked away so no one would see me. I could clean up around the house and get a job somewhere. Maybe Rush would let me sleep in this small unused room until I had enough money to move out. I didn't feel like I was imposing so badly back here. I'd find a grocery store tomorrow and use my twenty dollars for some food. Peanut butter and bread should get me through a week or so.

"This is perfect. I'm out of the way back here. Besides, Rush is calling my dad tomorrow and finding out when he will be home. Maybe my father has a plan. I don't know. Thank you though, I really appreciate the offer."

Grant looked around the room one more time and scowled. He wasn't happy about this room but I was relieved. It was sweet of him to care.

"I hate leaving you back here. It feels wrong." He looked back at me this time with a pleading sound to his voice.

"This is great. Much better than my truck would have been."

Grant frowned. "Truck? You were gonna sleep in your truck?"

"Yes. I was. This, however, gives me a little time to figure out what I'm gonna do next."

Grant ran a hand through his shaggy hair. "Will you promise me something?" he asked.

I wasn't one to make promises. What I knew of promises was that they were easily broken. I shrugged. It was the best I could do.

"If Rush makes you leave, call me."

I started to agree and realized I didn't have his phone number.

"Where's your phone so I can put my number in it?" he asked.

This was going to make me sound even more pathetic. "I don't have one."

Grant gaped at me, "You don't have a cell phone? No wonder you carry a damn gun." He reached into his pocket and pulled out what looked like a receipt. "You got a pen?"

I pulled one out of my purse and handed it to him.

He quickly scribbled his number down and then handed the paper and the pen to me. "Call me. I mean it."

I would never call him but it was nice that he was offering. I nodded. I hadn't promised anything.

"I hope you sleep okay in here." He looked around the small room with concern in his eyes. I would sleep wonderfully.

"I will," I assured him.

He nodded and stepped out of the room closing the door behind him. I waited until I heard him close the pantry door as well before I sat down on the bed beside my suitcase. This was good. I could work with this.

THREE

Even with no windows in the room to tell me if the sun was up, I knew I'd slept late. I had been exhausted but a long eight-hour drive and footsteps on the stairs for hours after I'd laid down kept me from sleeping. Stretching, I sat up and reached for the light switch on the wall. The small bulb lit the room and I reached under the bed to pull out my suitcase.

I needed a shower and I needed to use the restroom. Maybe everyone would still be asleep and I could sneak in and out of a bathroom without anyone noticing. Grant hadn't shown me where one was last night. This was all I'd been offered. Hopefully a quick shower wouldn't be pushing the limit.

I grabbed clean panties and a pair of black shorts and a sleeveless white top. If I was lucky, I'd get in and out of the shower and be cleaning up before Rush made his way downstairs.

I opened the door leading into the pantry then walked through the rows of shelves that held more food than anyone could possibly need. I slowly turned the doorknob and eased the door open. The kitchen light was off and the only light was the bright sun streaming in through the large windows overlooking the ocean. If I didn't need to pee so badly I would go enjoy the view a moment. But nature was calling and I had to go. The house was silent. Empty drinks littered the place, along with leftover food and some pieces of clothing. I could clean this up. If I proved to be useful I might get to stay until I could get a job and a paycheck or two.

I slowly opened the first door I came to, afraid it could be a bedroom. It was a walk-in closet. Closing it, I made my way back down the hall toward the stairs. If the only bathrooms were attached to bedrooms I was screwed. Except . . . maybe there was one that people used outside after being at the beach all day. Henrietta had to take showers and use the restroom too. Turning around I headed back to the kitchen and the two glass doors that had been standing open last night. Glancing around, I noticed a set of steps going down and underneath the house. I followed them.

At the bottom were two doors. I opened one and life jackets, surfboards and floats covered the walls. I went and opened the other one. Bingo.

A toilet was on one side and a small shower took up the other side of the room. Shampoo, conditioner and soap along with a fresh washcloth and a towel was on the small stool beside it. How convenient.

Once I was clean and dressed I hung the towel and bath cloth over the shower rod. This bathroom wasn't used often. I could use the same towel and washcloth all week and then wash them on the weekends. If I was here that long.

I closed the door behind me and headed back up the steps. The ocean air smelled wonderful. Once I got to the top, I stood at the railing and looked out over the water. Waves crashed onto the white sandy beach. It was the most beautiful thing I'd ever seen.

Mom and I had talked about seeing the ocean together one day. She'd seen it as a little girl and her memories weren't that great but she'd told me stories about it all my life. Every winter when it was cold, we would sit inside by the fire and plan our summer trip to the beach. We never were able to take it. First mom hadn't been able to afford it and then she'd been too sick. We still planned them anyway. It helped to dream big.

Now, here I stood staring at the waves we'd only dreamed about. It wasn't the fairytale vacation we'd planned but I was here seeing it for both of us.

"That view never gets old." Rush's deep drawl startled me. I spun around to see Rush leaning against the open door. Shirtless. Oh. My.

I couldn't form words. The only naked male chest I'd ever seen was Cain's. And that had been back before my mom got sick when I'd had time for dates and fun. Cain's sixteen-year-old chest had nothing on the broad, cut muscles in front of me. He had actual ripples in his stomach.

"Are you enjoying the view?" His amused tone didn't escape me. I blinked and lifted my eyes back up to see the smirk on his lips. Dangit. He'd caught me ogling him.

"Don't let me interrupt you. I was enjoying it myself," he replied, then took a sip from the coffee cup in his hand.

My face heated and I knew I was three kinds of red. Turning back around, I stared out at the ocean. How embarrassing. I was trying to get this guy to let me stay for a little while. Drooling was not the best move.

A low chuckle from behind me only made it worse. He was laughing at me. Fantastic.

"There you are. I missed you in bed this morning." A soft female coo came from behind me. Curiosity got the better of me and I turned around. A girl in nothing but her bra and panties was snuggling up to Rush's side and running a long pink fingernail down his chest. I couldn't blame her for wanting to touch that. I was pretty tempted myself.

"It's time for you to go," he replied taking her hand off his chest and stepping away from her. I watched as he pointed in the direction of the front door.

"What?" she replied. The confused expression on her face said she hadn't been expecting this.

"You got what you came here for, babe. You wanted me between your legs. You got it. Now I'm done."

The cold hard flatness in his voice startled me. Was he serious?

"You're kidding me!" the girl snapped and stomped her foot.

Rush shook his head and took another drink from his cup.

"You are not going to do this to me. Last night was amazing. You know it." The girl reached out for his arm and he quickly moved it out of the way.

"I warned you last night when you came to me begging and taking off your clothes that all it would ever be was one night of sex. Nothing more."

I shifted my attention back to the girl. Her face was in an angry snarl and she opened her mouth to argue but shut it again. With another stomp of her foot she stalked back inside the house.

I couldn't believe what I'd just seen. Was that the way people like this behaved? The only experience I'd had with relationships was with Cain. Although we'd never actually slept together he'd been careful and sweet with me. This was hard and cruel.

"So, how did you sleep last night?" Rush asked as if nothing had happened.

I tore my gaze off the door the girl had gone through and studied him. What had possessed that girl to sleep with someone who had told her it would be nothing more than sex? Sure, he had a body that underwear models were jealous of and those eyes of his could make a girl do crazy things. But still. He was so cruel.

"Do you do that often?" I asked before I could stop myself.

Rush cocked an eyebrow. "What? Ask people if they slept well?"

He knew what I was asking. He was avoiding it. It wasn't my business. I needed to stay out of the way so he would let me stay. Opening my mouth to scold him wasn't a good idea.

"Have sex with girls and then throw them out like trash?" I retorted. I closed my mouth, horrified as the words I'd just said echoed in my head. What was I doing? Trying to get tossed out?

Rush put his cup on the table beside him and sat down. He leaned back stretching out his long legs. Then he stared back up at me. "Do you always stick your nose where it doesn't belong?" he replied.

I wanted to get mad at him. But I couldn't. He was right. Who was I to point fingers? I didn't know the guy.

"Not normally, no. I'm sorry," I said, and hurried inside. I didn't want to give him a chance to throw me out too. I needed that bed under the stairs for at least two weeks.

I got busy picking up the empty glasses and bottles of beer. This place needed a cleaning and I could do that before I headed out to find a job. I just hoped he didn't throw parties like this every night. If he did, I wouldn't complain and who knows, after a few nights I might be able to sleep through anything.

"You don't have to do that. Henrietta will be here tomorrow."

I dropped the bottles I'd collected into the trash and then looked over at him. He was standing at the door again watching me.

"I just thought I'd help out."

Rush smirked. "I already have a housekeeper. I'm not looking to hire another one if that is what you're thinking."

I shook my head. "No. I know that. I was just trying to be helpful. You let me sleep in your house last night."

Rush walked over and stood in front of the counter crossing his arms over his chest. "About that. We need to talk."

Oh, crap. Here it goes. One night was all I was getting.

"Okay," I replied.

Rush frowned at me and I felt my heart rate increase. He wasn't about to bestow happy news.

"I don't like your father. He's a mooch. My mother always tends to find men like him. It's her talent. But I'm thinking you may already know this about him. Which makes me curious, why did you come to him for help if you knew what he was like?"

I'd like to tell him it was none of his business. Except the fact I'd needed his help made it his business. I couldn't expect him to let me sleep in his house and not explain things to him. He deserved to know why he was helping me. I didn't want him to think I was a mooch too.

"My mother just passed away. She had cancer. Three years' worth of treatments add up. The only thing we owned was the house my grandmother left us. I had to sell the house and everything else to pay off all my mother's medical bills. I haven't seen my dad since he walked out on us five years ago. But he's the only family I have left. I had no one else to ask for help. I need a place to stay until I can find a job and get a few paychecks.

Then I'll get my own place. I never intended to be around long. I knew my dad wouldn't want me here." I let out a hard laugh that I didn't feel. "Although, I never expected him to run off before I arrived."

Rush's steady gaze was still firmly directed at me. This was information I would have rather no one know. I used to talk to Cain about how my dad's abandonment had hurt. The loss of my sister and father had been hard on my mother and me. Then Cain had needed more and I couldn't be who he needed. I had a sick mother to take care of. I'd let Cain go so he could date other girls and have fun. I was just a weight around his neck. Our friendship had remained intact but I realized that the boy I once thought I'd loved had just been a childish emotion.

"I'm sorry to hear about your mom," Rush finally replied. "That's got to be rough. You said she was sick for three years. So since you were sixteen?"

I nodded, not sure what else to say. I didn't want his pity. Just a place to sleep.

"You're planning on getting a job and a place of your own." He wasn't asking a question. He was working through what I had told him. So I didn't reply.

"The room under the stairs is yours for one month. You should be able to find a job and get enough money together to find an apartment. Destin isn't too far from here and the cost of living is more affordable there. If our parents return before that time I expect your father will be able to help you out."

Letting out a sigh of relief I swallowed the lump in my throat. "Thank you."

Rush glanced back at the pantry that led to the room I was sleeping in. Then he looked back at me. "I've got some things to do. Good luck on the job hunt," Rush replied. He shoved off from the counter and walked away.

I had no fuel in my truck but I had a bed. I also had twenty dollars. I hurried to my room to get my purse and keys. I needed to find a job as quickly as possible.

FOUR

There was a note stuck under the windshield wiper of my truck. I pulled it out and read:

"Tank is full. Grant."

Grant had gotten me gasoline? My chest felt suddenly warm. That was so nice of him. Rush's words "mooch" rang in my ears and I realized I would need to pay Grant back as soon as possible. I would not be thought of as a mooch like my father.

Getting into the truck, I cranked it up easily and backed out of the driveway. Several cars were still outside, although not as many as last night. I wondered who all stayed the night. Would they always be here? I hadn't seen anyone this morning but Rush and the girl he'd run off.

Rush wasn't a very nice person but he was fair. I had to give him that. He was also sexy as hell. I'd just have to learn to overlook that. It should be easy enough. I didn't expect Rush would be hanging around me often. He didn't seem to like to be around me very much.

I'd decided that I'd get a job in Rosemary to save on gas. Then I could move out of Rush's house quicker. I had found a local newspaper and I'd circled several different jobs. Two were waitress jobs at local restaurants and I'd stopped in to apply. I had a feeling I would get a call back from one or both but I wasn't sure I wanted to work at either. I would if it was all that came available though. It just didn't look like the tips would be that good and with a job like that you need the tips. I also stopped by the local pharmacy to apply for the front register position but they had already filled it. Then I'd gone by the local pediatrician's office to apply for the receptionist job but they wanted experience and I had none.

There was one last job I'd circled and I had put it off because I figured it would be a harder job to snag; a serving position at the local country club. It paid seven more dollars an hour plus the tips would be much better. I could be out on my own even sooner. Plus, there were benefits. Health insurance would be great.

The help wanted ad had said to come to the main offices behind the golf course clubhouse to apply. I followed the directions and parked my truck beside a fancy Volvo. I adjusted the rearview mirror to check my face. I had picked up a small tube of mascara while I was at the pharmacy. Just a little mascara helped my face look older. I ran a hand through my pale blonde hair and said a quick prayer that I was able to get this job.

I had changed out of my shorts and sleeveless top when I'd gone to get my purse. I figured a sundress was more likely to help me get a job. Rush said I looked like a kid. I wanted to look older. The mascara and dress seemed to help.

I didn't bother locking the truck. It wasn't in danger of being stolen here. Not when most of the cars parked nearby cost over sixty thousand dollars. The steps up to the office door were few. Taking one last deep breath I opened the door and stepped inside.

A petite woman with a short brown bob and a pair of wire-rimmed glasses was walking across the reception room when I stepped inside. She glanced over at me as she made her way to one of the offices but stopped in her tracks when she saw me. She gave a quick glance at the rest of me and then nodded her head in my direction.

"You here for a job?" she asked commandingly.

I nodded, "Yes, ma'am. I'm here about a server position."

She gave me a tight smile. "Good. You have the appeal. The members will overlook mistakes with a face like that. Can you drive a golf cart and can you open a bottle of beer with a bottle opener?"

I nodded.

"You're hired. I need someone on the course right now. Follow me; we'll get you changed into uniform."

I didn't argue. When she spun back around and started stalking toward another room I followed behind her. She was a woman on a mission. She opened a door and walked inside.

"You wear a size three in shorts? Your top is going to be smaller than what you're wearing. The men will love that though. They like larger chest sizes. Let's see . . ." She was talking about my boobs. That was awkward. She grabbed a pair of white shorts off the rack and shoved them at me. Then she grabbed a pale blue polo shirt from the rack. "That's a small top. It needs to be tight. We are a classy establishment here but our men like to have eye candy too. Therefore, we offer it up in a pair of white shorts and tight polos. Don't worry about paperwork. I'll have you fill all that out after work. You do this for a week and do it well and we will see about moving you into the dining room. We are short-staffed in there too. Faces like yours aren't easy to find. Now, get changed and I'll be waiting to take you out to the drinks cart."

Two hours later, I'd stopped at all eighteen holes on the golf course twice and sold out of drinks. The golfers all wanted to ask me if I was new and comment on my excellent service. I wasn't an idiot. I saw the way the older men were leering at me. Thankfully, they all seemed careful not to cross any lines.

The lady who hired me had finally told me her name when she'd all but pushed me up onto the cart and sent me off. She was Darla Lowry. She was in charge of hiring staff. She was also a whirlwind. She'd told me that I was to return in four hours or when I ran out of drinks, whichever came first. I'd run out of drinks in two hours.

I walked inside the office and Darla stuck her head out of one of the rooms. "You're back already?" she asked, walking out with her hands on her hips.

"Yes ma'am. I ran out of drinks."

Her eyebrows shot up, "All of them?"

I nodded. "Yes. All of them."

A smile crossed her stern face and she let out a laugh. "Well, I'll be damned. I knew they'd like you but those horny men were willing to buy whatever you had just to get you to stay longer."

I wasn't sure that was the case. It was hot out there. Every time I stopped at a hole the golfers looked relieved.

"Come on, I'll show you where to restock. You need to keep serving until the sun goes down. Then come back in here and we will get that paperwork filled out."

It was dark by the time I arrived back at Rush's house. I'd been gone all day. The extra cars in the driveway were now gone. The three-car garage was closed and one expensive red convertible was parked outside of it. I made sure to park my truck out of the way. Rush might have more friends coming over and I didn't want my truck to be a problem. I was exhausted. I just wanted to go to bed.

I stopped at the door and wondered if I should knock or just go inside. Rush had said I could stay here for a month. Surely that meant I didn't have to knock every time I came back.

I turned the knob and walked inside. The entrance was empty and surprisingly clean. Someone had picked up the mess in here already. The marble floor even looked shiny. I heard a television coming from the large open living room. There wasn't a lot of other noise. I made my way to the kitchen. I had a bed waiting on me. I'd really like a shower but I hadn't talked to Rush about which shower I was supposed to use yet and I didn't want to bother him tonight. I'd just sneak out tomorrow and use the same one I'd used this morning when I woke up.

The smell of garlic and cheese met my nose as I stepped into the kitchen. My stomach growled in response. I had a pack of peanut butter crackers in my purse and a small container of milk that I'd bought at a service station on my way home. I'd made some money today in tips but I couldn't waste my money on food. I needed to be save everything I could.

There was a covered pan on the stove and an open wine bottle sitting on the counter. Two plates with the remnants of a tantalizing pasta dish were also on the counter. Rush had company.

A moan came from outside followed by a loud noise.

I walked over to the window but as soon as the moon hit the backside of Rush's naked bottom I froze. It was a very nice naked bottom. A very, very nice one. Although I hadn't really seen a guy's naked backside before. I let my eyes travel up his back and the tattoos that covered it surprised me. I couldn't tell what they were exactly. The moonlight wasn't enough and he was moving.

His hips moved back and forth and I noticed the two long legs that he had pressed to his sides. The loud moaning noise came again as he moved faster. I covered my mouth and took a step back. Rush was having sex. Outside. On his porch. I couldn't turn away from it. His hands grabbed the legs on either side of him and he pushed them open further. A loud cry caused me to jump. Two hands came around his back and long nails clawed at the tattoos that covered the tanned skin.

I shouldn't be watching this. Shaking my head to clear it I turned and hurried into the pantry and my hidden bedroom. I couldn't think about Rush that way. He was sexy enough. Seeing him actually having sex made my heart do funny things. It wasn't like I wanted to be one of those girls he had sex with and then tossed away. Seeing his body like that and hearing how he was making the girl feel made me just a little jealous. I'd never known that. Being nineteen years old and still a virgin was sad. Cain had said he loved me but when I'd needed him the most he'd wanted a girlfriend who could sneak out and have sex without having to worry about her sick mother. He'd wanted a normal high school experience. I'd hindered that so I'd let him go.

When I'd left yesterday morning to come here he had begged me to stay. He'd claimed he loved me. That he'd never gotten over me. That every girl he'd ever been with was just a poor substitute. I couldn't believe all that. I'd cried myself to sleep alone and scared too many nights. I'd needed someone to hold me. He hadn't been there then. He didn't understand love.

I closed the door to my bedroom and collapsed on the bed. I didn't even pull back the covers. I needed sleep. I had to be at work at nine in the morning. I smiled to myself because I was thankful. I had a bed and a job.

FIVE

The sun was exceptionally bright. Darla didn't want me to pull my hair up in a ponytail. She seemed to think the men liked it down. Unfortunately for me, it was so freaking hot. I reached into the cooler for an ice cube and rubbed it down my neck and let it slip down into my shirt. I was almost to the fifteenth hole for the third time today.

This morning no one had been awake when I'd come out of my room. The empty plates had still been sitting on the bar. I'd cleaned it up and thrown out the food in the pan he'd left out all night. It made me sad to see it wasted. It had smelled so good last night when I'd come home.

Then I'd thrown away the empty wine bottle and found the glasses outside on the table beside where I'd watched Rush going at it with the unknown female. After putting the dirty dishes in the dishwasher I'd turned it on and wiped down the counters and stovetop.

I doubted Rush noticed but it made me feel better about sleeping there for free. I pulled up beside the group of golfers at the fifteenth hole. They were a younger crowd. I'd seen them when they'd been on the third hole. They bought a lot and they were really good tippers. So I put up with their flirtatious behavior. It wasn't like one of them would really date the cart girl at the golf course. I wasn't an idiot.

"There she is," one of the guys called out as I pulled up beside them and smiled.

"Ah, my favorite girl is back. It's hotter than hell girl. I need a cold one. Maybe two."

I parked the cart and got out to go around the back and take their orders.

"You want another Miller?" I asked him proud of myself for remembering his last order.

"Yeah, baby, I do." He winked and closed the distance between us making me a little uncomfortable.

"Hey, I want something too Jace. Back off the goods," another guy said and I kept my smile on my face as I handed him his beer and he handed me a twenty dollar bill. "Keep the change."

"Thank you," I replied, tucking the money into my pocket. I glanced up at the other guys. "Who's next?"

"Me," a guy with short curly blond hair and pretty blue eyes said, waving around a bill.

"You want a Corona, right?" I asked reaching into the cooler and pulling out the drink he'd ordered last time.

"I think I'm in love. She's gorgeous and she remembers what beer I drink. Then she opens the damn thing for me." I could tell he was teasing as he stuck a bill in my hand and took the beer from me. "Change is yours, beautiful."

I noticed the fifty as I stuck it into my pocket. These guys really didn't mind throwing money away. That was a ridiculous tip. I felt like telling him not to give me so much but I decided against it. They probably tipped like this all the time.

"What's your name?" one asked and I turned to see the dark haired guy with an olive complexion waiting to give his order and hear my answer.

"Blaire," I replied reaching into the cooler for the fancy beer he'd requested. I popped the top and handed it to him.

"You got a boyfriend, Blaire?" he asked, taking the drink from me while running a finger along the side of my hand in a caress.

"Um, no," I replied, not sure if it might have been better to lie in this situation.

The guy took a step toward me and held out his hand with the payment and tip inside of it. "I'm Woods," he replied.

"It's, uh, nice to meet you, Woods," I stammered in reply. The intense look in his dark eyes made me nervous. He could be dangerous and he reeked of expensive cologne. Expertly bred. He was one of the beautiful people and he knew it. What was he doing flirting with me?

"Not fair, Woods. Back off, bro. You're going all out with this one. Just 'cause your daddy owns the joint doesn't mean you get first dibs," the blond with curls kidded. I think he was kidding.

Woods ignored his friend and kept his focus on me. "What time do you get off work?"

Uh-oh. If I understood them correctly then Woods' daddy was my ultimate boss. I didn't need to be spending time the owner's son. That would be a very bad thing.

"I work until close," I explained, and handed the last of the four his beer and took his money.

"Why don't you let me pick you up and take you for something to eat?" Woods said, standing very close to me now. If I turned around he would be only a breath away.

"It's hot and I'm already exhausted. All I will want to do is get a shower and crash."

Warm breath tickled my ear and I shivered as beads of sweat rolled down my back. "Are you scared of me? Don't be. I'm harmless."

I wasn't sure what to do about him. I wasn't good with the flirting and I was pretty sure that was what he was doing. No one had flirted with me in years. Once I broke up with Cain, my days had been consumed with school and then my mom. I had no time for anything else. Guys didn't bother with me.

"You don't scare me. I'm just not used to this kind of thing," I replied apologetically. I didn't know how to respond properly.

"What kind of thing?" he asked curiously. I finally turned around to face him.

"Guys. And flirting. At least, I think that is what is happening." I sounded like an idiot. The smile that slowly stretched across Woods face made me want to crawl under the golf cart and hide. I was so out of my league.

"Yes, this is definitely flirting. And how is it that someone as fucking unbelievably hot as you is not used to this kind of thing?"

I tensed at his words and shook my head. I needed to get to the sixteenth hole. "I've just been busy the past few years. If, uh, you don't need anything else the golfers on the sixteenth hole are probably angry with me by now."

Woods nodded and took a step back. "I'm not done with you. Not by a long shot. But for right now I'll let you get back to work."

I hurried back to the driver's side of the cart and climbed in. The next hole was a bunch of retired men. I had never looked more forward to being leered at by old guys in my life but at least they didn't flirt.

When I walked out to my truck that evening I was relieved to see no sign of Woods. I should have known he was just teasing the help. I had made a couple of hundred dollars in tips today and I decided that treating myself to an actual meal was okay. I pulled into the drive-thru at McDonalds and ordered a cheeseburger and fries. I ate them happily on the way back to Rush's. There was no car outside tonight.

I wouldn't walk in on him having sex tonight. Then again, he might have brought someone here in his car. I walked inside and stopped in the foyer. No television. No sound at all, but the door had been unlocked. I hadn't had to use the hidden key he'd told me about.

I'd sweated too much today. I had to have a shower before I went to bed. I stepped into the kitchen and checked the front porch to make sure it was free of any sexual escapades. Getting a shower would be easy.

I ducked into my room and grabbed the old pair of Cain's boxers and a tank top that I slept in at night. Cain had given them to me when we were young and silly. He'd wanted me to sleep in something that was his. I'd been sleeping in them every since. Although now they were much tighter than they had been then. I'd developed curves since the age of fifteen.

I took a deep breath of the ocean air as I stepped outside. This was my third night here and I had yet to actually make it down to the water. I'd come home so tired that I hadn't had the energy to go out there. I went down the steps and put my pajamas in the bathroom before slipping off my tennis shoes.

The sand was still warm from the sun's heat. I walked across it in the darkness until the water's edge rushed up to meet me. The cold startled me and I sucked in a breath but let the salt water cover my feet.

My mom's smile as she told me about the time she'd played in the ocean flashed in my memory and I tilted my head up to heaven and smiled. I was finally here. I was here for both of us.

A sound to the left broke into my thoughts. I turned to look down the beach just as the moonlight broke free of the clouds and Rush was spotlighted in the darkness. Running.

Once again, he was shirtless. The shorts he was wearing hung low on his narrow hips and I was mesmerized by the way his body looked as he ran toward me. I wasn't sure if I should move or if he was done. His feet slowed and then he came to a stop beside me. The sweat on his chest glistened in the soft light. Oddly enough I wanted to reach out and touch it. Something that a body like his made couldn't be gross. It was impossible.

"You're back," he said as he took a few deep breaths.

"I just got off work," I replied, trying hard to keep my eyes on his and not his chest.

"So you got a job?"

"Yes. Yesterday."

"Where at?"

I wasn't sure how I felt about telling him too much. He wasn't a friend. And it was obvious I'd never consider him family. Our parents might be married but he didn't seem to want to have anything to do with my father or me.

"Kerrington Country Club," I replied.

Rush's eyebrows shot up and he took a step closer to me. He slipped a hand under my chin and tilted my face up. "You're wearing mascara," he said, studying me.

"Yes, I am," I pulled my chin out of his grasp. He might be letting me sleep at his house but I didn't like him touching me.

Or maybe I did like him touching me and that was the problem. I didn't want to like him touching me.

"It makes you look more your age." He stepped back and did a slow appraisal of my clothing.

"You're the cart girl at the golf course," he said simply looking back up at me.

"How did you know?" I asked.

He waved a hand at me. "The outfit. Tight little white shorts and polo shirts. It's the uniform."

I was glad for the darkness. I was positive I was blushing.

"You're making a fucking killing aren't you?" he asked in an amused tone.

I'd made over five hundred dollars in tips in two days. That wasn't a killing to him but to me it was.

I shrugged. "You will be relieved to know that I'll be out of here in less than a month."

He didn't respond right away. I should probably leave and go get my shower. I started to say something when he took a step closer to me. "I probably should be. Relieved that is. Real fucking relieved. But, I'm not. I'm not relieved, Blaire," he paused and leaned down to whisper in my ear, "why is that?"

I wanted to reach out and grab his arms to keep from crumpling to the ground in a heap of mush. But I refrained.

"Keep your distance from me, Blaire. You don't want to get too close. Last night." He swallowed loudly. "Last night is haunting me. Knowing you were watching. It drives me crazy. So, stay away. I'm doing my best to stay away from you." He turned and jogged back up to the house as I stood there trying to keep from melting into a puddle on the sand.

What had he meant by that? How had he known I'd seen them? When I saw the door to the house close behind him I walked back and got my shower. His words were going to keep me up most of the night.

SIX

Staying away from Rush wasn't exactly easy since we were living under the same roof. Even if he attempted to keep his distance, we were still bumping into each other. He also avoided eye contact with me but that only made me more fascinated with him.

Two days later after our talk on the beach, I stepped into the kitchen after eating my peanut butter sandwich and was greeted by yet another half naked female. Her hair was a mess but even in its unbrushed state she was attractive. I hated girls like that.

The girl turned to look at me. Her surprised expression quickly switched to annoyed. She batted both of her brown eyes and then placed a hand on her hip. "Did you just come out of the pantry?"

"Yes. Did you just come out of Rush's bed?" I replied. It was out of my mouth before I could stop myself. Rush had already informed me that his sex life was not my business. I needed to shut up.

The girl raised both her perfectly plucked eyebrows and then an amused grin crossed her lips. "No. Not that I wouldn't get in his bed if he'd let me but don't tell Grant that." She waved a hand as if to shoo away a fly. "Never mind. He probably already knows."

I was confused. "So, you just got out of Grant's bed?" I asked realizing that once again this was not my business. But Grant didn't live here so I was curious.

The girl ran her hand through her messy mop of brown curls and sighed. "Yep. Or at least his old bed."

"His old bed?" I repeated.

Movement in the doorway caught my attention and my eyes locked with Rush's. He was watching me with a smirk on his lips. Great. He'd heard me prying. I wanted to look away and pretend like I hadn't just asked the girl if she'd been in his bed. The knowing gleam in his eyes told me it was no use.

"Please don't let me stop you, Blaire. Continue to give Grant's guest the third degree. I'm sure he won't mind," Rush drawled. He crossed his arms over his chest and leaned against the doorframe as if he was getting comfortable.

I ducked my head and walked over to the garbage to dust the bread crumbs from my fingers while I gathered my thoughts. I did not want to continue this conversation while Rush listened. It made me seem all too interested in him. Something he did not want.

"Good morning, Rush, thanks for letting us crash here last night. Grant had drank entirely too much to drive all the way back to his place," the girl said.

Oh. So that's the story. Crap. Why had I let my curiosity get the best of me?

"Grant knows he has a room when he wants it," Rush replied. I could see him shove off from the doorframe and walk over to the counter from the corner of my eye. His attention was on me. Why couldn't he let this go? I would leave quietly.

"Well, uh, I guess I'll run back upstairs then," the girl's voice sounded unsure. Rush didn't respond and I didn't look back at either of them. The girl took that as her cue to leave and I waited until I heard her footsteps on the stairs before glancing over at Rush.

"Curiosity killed the kitty, sweet Blaire," Rush whispered as he walked closer to me. "Did you think I'd had another sleep over? Hmmm? Trying to decide if she had been in my bed all night?"

I swallowed hard but didn't say anything.

"Who I sleep with isn't your business. Haven't we gone over this before?"

I managed to nod. If he would just let me go I'd never speak to another girl that showed up in his house.

Rush reached out and wound a lock of my hair around his finger. "You don't want to know me. You may think you do but you don't. I promise."

If he wasn't so dang gorgeous and right under my nose then

it would be easier to believe this. But the more he pushed me away the more intrigued I became.

"You aren't what I expected. I wish you were. It'd be so much easier," he said in a low voice then dropped my hair then turned and walked away. When the door leading to the back porch closed I let out the breath I'd been holding.

What did he mean? What had he expected?

That night when I got home from work, Rush wasn't there.

I opened my eyes and turned to look at the small alarm clock on the nightstand. It was after nine in the morning. I had really slept in. Stretching, I reached up and turned on the light. I'd showered last night so I was clean. I had made over one thousand dollars this week. I decided I could start looking at apartments today. This time next week I should be able to get a place of my own.

I ran my hands through my hair and tried to tame it before getting up. I was going to go lay on the beach for a little while this morning. I hadn't done that yet. Today I would enjoy the ocean and sunshine.

I pulled my suitcase out from under my bed and searched inside for my white and pink bikini. It was the only one I owned. To be honest, it had been used very little. The white lace pattern and pink piping looked good with my coloring.

Pulling it on I decided it was skimpier than I remembered. Or my body had changed since the last time I had worn it. I pulled a tank top out of the suitcase to slip it on over the bikini and grabbed my sunblock. I had bought it after my first day of work. Sunblock was a must for my job.

I turned my light off and stepped into the pantry and then into the kitchen. "Holy hell. Who is that?" a younger guy asked startling me as I stepped into the light. I glanced from the stranger sitting at the bar gawking at me to the fridge where Grant stood smiling.

"You come walking out of that room dressed like that every morning?" Grant asked.

I hadn't expected anyone to be in here. "Um, no. Normally I'm dressed for work," I replied as a low whistle came from the younger boy at the bar. He couldn't be any older than sixteen.

"Ignore the hormone ridden idiot at the bar. That's Will. His mother and Georgianna are sisters. So in some screwed up roundabout way he is my younger cousin. He showed up here last night after running away again for the hundredth damn time and Rush called me to come get him and take his crazy ass home."

Rush. Why did the sound of his name make my heart race? Because he was unfairly perfect. That was why. I shook my head to clear my Rush thoughts. "It's nice to meet you, Will. I'm Blaire. Rush has taken pity on me until I can get my own place."

"Hey, you can come home with me. I won't make you sleep under the stairs," Will offered.

I couldn't help but smile. This kind of innocent flirting I understood.

"Thank you but I don't think your mother will appreciate that. I'm fine under the stairs. The bed is comfortable and I don't have to sleep with my gun."

Grant chuckled and Will's eyes went wide. "You've gotta gun?" Will asked in an awed voice.

"Now, you've gone and done it. I better get him out of here before he falls anymore in love," Grant replied, taking the cup he'd just filled up with coffee. He headed for the door saying, "Come on Will, before I go wake up Rush and you have to deal with his ornery ass."

Will glanced at Grant then back at me as if he were torn. It was cute.

"Now, Will," Grant said in a more demanding tone.

"Hey, Grant," I called before he got to the door.

He turned back to look at me, "Yeah?"

"Thanks for the gas. I'm paying you back as soon as I get my check."

Grant shook his head, "No, you're not. I'll be insulted. But you're welcome." He winked then shot Will a warning glare before leaving the kitchen.

I waved goodbye to Will. I'd deal with how to pay Grant back without insulting him later. There had to be a way. Right now, I had another plan. I made my way to the doors leading outside. It was time to enjoy my first real day on the beach.

I stretched out on the towel I'd borrowed from the bathroom. I'd have to wash it tonight. It was the only one I had to dry off with and now I was getting it covered in sand. It was so worth it.

The beach was quiet. We weren't near other houses so this stretch of the beach was empty. Feeling brave, I pulled the tank top off and tucked it under my head. Then I closed my eyes and let the sound of the ocean waves crashing against the shore lull me back to sleep.

"Please tell me you have sunblock on," a deep voice washed over me and I leaned toward it. The clean masculine scent was yummy. I needed to get closer.

Opening my eyes, I blinked at the bright sun and covered my eyes to see Rush sitting down beside me. His eyes were studying me. Any warmth or humor in his voice I might have imagined was missing.

"You are wearing sunblock, aren't you?"

I managed to nod and then pulled myself up to a sitting position.

"Good. I'd hate to see that smooth creamy skin turn pink."

He thought my skin was smooth and creamy. It sounded like a compliment but I wasn't sure saying thank you was appropriate.

"I, uh, put some on before I came out here."

He continued to stare at me. I fought the urge to reach for my shirt and slip it on over my bikini. I didn't have the kind of body the girls I'd seen him with did. I didn't like feeling as if he were comparing me.

"You not working today?" he finally asked.

I shook my head. "It's my day off."

"How's the job going?"

He was being nice, kind of. At least he wasn't avoiding me. As silly as it seemed, I wanted his attention. There was this draw I had to him that I couldn't explain. The more he kept his distance the more I wanted to get closer. He tilted his head and cocked an eyebrow like he was waiting on me to say something.

Oh wait. He'd asked me a question. Dang those silver eyes of his. It was hard to concentrate. "Uh, what?" I asked feeling my face heat up.

He chuckled, "How is the job going?" he asked slowly.

I had to stop making an idiot out of myself around him. I straightened my shoulders, "It's going good. I like it."

Rush smirked and glanced out over the water, "I bet you do."

I paused and thought about that comment then asked, "What is that supposed to mean?"

Rush let his gaze trail down my body then back up. I was regretting not putting my tank top back on. "You know what you look like, Blaire. Not to mention that damn sweet smile of yours. The male golfers are paying you well."

He was right about the tips. He was also making me breathe funny looking at me like that. I wanted him to like what he saw but then I was also terrified of the outcome. What if he did change his mind about keeping his distance? Could I keep up?

We sat in silence for awhile as he stared straight ahead. I could tell he was thinking about something. His jaw was clenched tight and there was a frown line creasing his forehead. I thought back to what all I'd said. I couldn't think of anything that would upset him.

"How long ago did your mom pass away?" he asked, turning his gaze back to me.

I didn't want to talk about my mom. Not to him. But ignoring his question was rude. "Thirty-six days ago."

His jaw worked as if he was angry about something and his frown line got deeper. "Did your dad know she was sick?"

Another question I didn't want to answer. "Yes. He knew. I also called him the day she passed away. He didn't answer. I left a message." The fact he never returned my call hurt too bad to admit.

"Do you hate him?" Rush asked.

I wanted to hate him. He had only caused pain in my life since the day my sister had died. But it was hard. He was the only family I had. "Sometimes," I replied honestly.

Rush nodded and reached over and hooked his pinky through mine. He didn't say anything but at that moment he didn't have to. That one small connection said enough. Maybe I didn't know Rush well but he was getting under my skin.

"I'm having a party tonight. It's Nan, my sister's birthday. I always give her a party. It may not be your scene but you're invited to attend if you want to."

His sister? He had a sister? I thought he was an only child. Wasn't Nan the girl who had been so rude the night I'd arrived?

"You have a sister?"

Rush shrugged, "Yeah."

Why had Grant said he was an only child? I waited for him to explain but he didn't elaborate. So I decided to ask.

"Grant said you were an only child."

Rush tensed. Then shook his head as he finger left mine and turned to look out at the water. "Grant really has no business telling you my business. No matter how damn bad he wants in your panties." Rush stood up and didn't look back at me as he turned and headed back to the house.

Something about Nan was off limits. I had no idea what it was but it was definitely off limits. I shouldn't have been so nosy. I stood up and headed out to the water. It was hot and I needed something to get my mind off Rush. Every time I let my guard down a little around him he reminded me why I needed to keep it firmly in place. The guy was strange. Sexy, gorgeous and delicious but strange.

I sat on my bed listening to the laughter and music in the house. I'd changed my mind about attending this party all day. The last time I had decided to go I'd put on the only nice dress I still owned. It was a red dress that hugged my chest and hips then hung in a short baby doll cut around my mid-thigh. I'd bought this dress when Cain had invited me to Senior Prom. Then he'd been nominated for prom king and Grace Anne Henry had been nominated prom queen. She'd wanted to go to the prom with him and he'd called and asked me if it would be okay if he went with her instead. Everyone had said they would win and he thought it would be cool if they were there together. I'd agreed with him and hung my dress back in my closet. That night I'd rented two movies and made brownies. Mom and I had watched romantic comedies and eaten brownies until we were stuffed. It was one of the last times I remember her not being so sick from chemo that she could actually eat treats like brownies.

Tonight I had pulled the dress out of my bag. It wasn't expensive by these people's standards. It was actually pretty simple. The red material was soft chiffon. I glanced down at my mom's silver heels that I'd kept. They had been the ones she'd worn the day of her wedding. I had always loved them. She never wore them again but they were kept in a box wrapped up tightly.

I risked a big chance of going out there and being humiliated. I didn't fit in with them. I'd never fit in at my high school either. My life was just one big awkward moment. I needed to learn to fit in. To walk away from the awkward girl who was left out in high school because she had bigger issues.

Standing up, I ran my hands over my dress to get out any wrinkles from sitting there thinking over the wisdom of joining the party. I would walk out there. Maybe get a drink and see if anyone spoke to me. If it was a complete disaster, I could always run back in here, put on my pajamas and curl up in bed. This was a good small step for me.

Opening the pantry door, I stepped into the kitchen very grateful that no one was in there. Walking out of the pantry would be slightly hard to explain. I could hear Grant's voice laughing loudly and talking to someone in the living room. He would talk to me. I could ease into this with Grant. Taking a deep breath, I walked out of the kitchen and down the hall into the foyer. White roses and silver ribbons were everywhere. It reminded me of a wedding instead of a birthday party. The front door opened startling me. I stopped and watched as familiar dark smoky eyes met mine. My face felt warm as Woods' eyes took a long slow appraisal of me.

"Blaire," he said, when his eyes finally made their way back to my face. "I didn't think it was possible for you to get any sexier. I was wrong."

"Hell, yeah girl. You clean up real nice." The guy with curly blond hair and blue eyes smiled at me. I couldn't remember his name. Had he even told me?

"Thank you," I managed to croak out. I was being awkward again. This was my chance to fit in. I needed to work on that.

"I didn't know Rush had started golfing again. Or are you here with someone else?" Confused, it took me a moment to understand Woods' meaning. When I realized that he thought I was here with someone who I had met at work I grinned. That wasn't the case at all.

"I'm not here with anyone. Rush is um . . . well Rush's mother is married to my father." There that explained it.

Woods' slow easy grin got bigger as he walked toward me. "Is that so? He is making his stepsister work at the country club? Tsk tsk. The boy has no manners. If I had a sister that looked like you I'd keep her locked up . . . all the time," He paused and reached up to brush his thumb across my cheek. "I'd stay with you of course. Wouldn't want you to be lonely."

He was definitely flirting. Heavily. I was way out of my league with this one. He was too experienced. I needed some space.

"Those legs of yours should come with a warning. Impossible not to touch," his voice lowered a notch and I glanced over his shoulder to see that blondie had left us.

"Are you . . . are you friends with Rush or uh, Nannette?" I asked remembering the name Grant had used to introduce us the first night.

Woods shrugged, "Nan and I have a complicated friendship. Rush and I have known each other our entire lives." His hand slid behind my back. "I'm betting like hell Nan isn't a fan of yours, though."

I wasn't sure. We hadn't really had any contact since that first night. "We don't really know each other."

Woods frowned, "Really? That's odd."

"Woods! You're here," a female squealed as she entered the room. He turned his head to see a red headed girl with long thick curls and a curvy body barely covered with black satin. This would be his distraction. I started to step away and go back toward the kitchen. My moment of bravery was now gone.

Woods' hand clamped down on my hip, firmly holding me in place. "Laney," was all that Woods said in response. Her big brown eyes shifted from him to me. I watched helplessly as she took in his hand settled on my hip. This was not what I wanted. I needed to fit in.

"Who is she?" the girl snapped her eyes now glaring at me.

"This is Blaire. Rush's new sister," Woods replied in a bored tone.

The girl's eyes narrowed and then she laughed. "No, she isn't. She's wearing a cheap ass dress and even cheaper shoes. This girl, whoever she says she is, is lying to you. But then you were always weak when it came to a pretty face, weren't you, Woods?"

I really should have stayed in my room.

SEVEN

"Why don't you go back to the party and find some stupid male to sharpen your claws on, Laney?"

Woods moved toward the door where the majority of the party was going on with his hand still firmly on my hip forcing me to go with him.

"I think I should just go to my room. I shouldn't have come out here tonight," I said, trying to stop our entrance into the party. I didn't need to walk in there with Woods. Something told me it was a bad idea.

"Why don't you show me to your room? I'd like to escape too."

I shook my head. "Not enough room for both of us."

Woods laughed and bent his head to say something in my ear as my eyes locked with Rush's silver gaze. He was watching me closely. He didn't look happy. Had his invite today been out of courtesy and not truly intended? Had I misunderstood?

"I need to leave. I don't think Rush wants me here." I turned to look up at Woods and stepped out of his embrace.

"Nonsense. I'm sure he is entirely too busy to worry about what you're doing. Besides, why wouldn't he want you at his other sister's party?"

There was that sister thing again. Why had Grant told me that Rush had no siblings? Nan was obviously his sister.

"I, uh, well, he doesn't actually claim me as family. I'm just the unwanted relative of his mother's new husband. I'm actually just here for a couple more weeks until I can move out on my own. I'm not a wanted resident in this house." I forced a smile, hoping Woods would get the picture and let me go.

"There is nothing about you that is unwanted. Even Rush isn't that damn blind," Woods said, closing in on me again as I backed away.

"Come here, Blaire." Rush's demanding tone came from behind me as a large hand slipped around my arm and pulled me back against him. "I didn't expect you to come tonight." The warning in his tone told me I had misunderstood his invite. He hadn't truly meant it.

"I'm sorry. I thought you said I could come," I whispered, embarrassed that Woods was hearing this. And others were watching it. The one time I decide to be brave and step out of my shell and this happens.

"I hadn't expected you to show up dressed like that," he replied with a deadly calm. His eyes were still directed at Woods.

What was so wrong with my clothes? My mom had sacrificed for me to have this dress and I'd never gotten to wear it. Sixty dollars was a lot of money for us when she'd bought it. I was sick of this stupid bunch of spoiled brats acting like I was dressed in something repulsive. I loved this dress. I loved these shoes. My parents had been happy and in love once. These shoes were a part of that. Damn them all to hell.

I jerked free of Rush and headed back to the kitchen. If he didn't want me in here for his friends to laugh at then he should have said so. Instead, he'd made me feel like a fool.

"What is your fucking problem, man?" Woods asked angrily. I didn't look back. I hoped they got in a fight. I hoped Woods busted Rush's obnoxiously perfect nose. I doubted it because although Rush was one of them he looked rougher around the edges.

"Blaire, wait," Grant called out and I wanted to ignore him but right now he was the closest thing I had to a friend here. I slowed down when I reached the hallway away from all the onlookers and let Grant catch up to me.

"That wasn't what you think in there," Grant said, coming up behind me. I wanted to laugh. He was very blinded where his brother was concerned.

"Doesn't matter. I shouldn't have come. I should have known he hadn't meant that invitation. I wish he'd just told me to stay in my room like he wanted me to. I don't understand word games," I snapped and stalked into the kitchen and straight to the pantry.

"He has issues. I'll give him that, but he was protecting you in his weird screwed up way," Grant said as my hand met the cold brass handle on the pantry door.

"Keep believing the best in him, Grant. That's what good brothers do," I replied and jerked the door open and closed it behind me. After a few deep breaths to ease the ache in my chest I went into my room and sank down onto the bed.

Parties were not my thing. That was the second one I'd ever been to and the first one hadn't been much better. Actually it was probably worse. I'd gone to surprise Cain and I'd been the one surprised. He'd been in Jamie Kirkman's bedroom with her naked breast in his mouth. They hadn't been having sex but they were definitely working their way up to it. I'd closed the door quietly behind me and left through the back door. Some people saw me and knew what I'd walked into. Cain had shown up at my house an hour later begging me to forgive him and crying while on his knees.

I'd loved him since I was thirteen years old and he'd given me my first kiss. I couldn't hate him. I just let him go. That was the end of our relationship. I eased his conscience and we had remained friends. Sometimes he had broken down and told me he loved me and wanted me back but for the most part he had a different girl in the back of his mustang every weekend. I was just a childhood memory.

Tonight no one had betrayed me. I'd just been humiliated. Reaching down I slipped off my mother's shoes and placed them safely back in the box she'd always kept them in. Then I put them back into my suitcase. I shouldn't have worn those tonight. The next time I wore her shoes would be special. It would be for someone special.

The same went for this dress. When I put it back on I would wear it for someone who loved me and thought I was beautiful. The price tag on my dress wouldn't matter. I reached up to unzip it when the door opened and the small doorway was filled with Rush. A very angry Rush.

He didn't say anything and I let my hands fall back to my side. I wouldn't be taking my dress off just yet. He stepped inside and closed the door behind him. He was too much for this small room. I had to back up and sit down on the bed so that he could fit without us touching.

"How do you know Woods?" he snarled.

Confused, I stared up at him and wondered why he didn't like me knowing Woods. Weren't they friends? Was that it? He didn't want me around his friends. "His dad owns the country club. He golfs. I serve him drinks."

"Why did you wear that?" he asked in a cold hard voice.

That was the last straw. I stood back up then inched higher on my tiptoes so that I was in his face. "Because my mother bought it for me to wear. I was stood up and never got the chance. Tonight you invited me and I wanted to fit in. So I wore the nicest thing I had. I'm sorry that it wasn't quite nice enough. You know what though? I don't give a shit. You and your uppity spoiled friends all need to get over yourselves."

I pushed his chest with my finger and glared at him daring him to say one more word about my dress.

Rush opened his mouth then closed his eyes tightly and shook his head. "Fuck!" he growled. Then his eyes flew open and his hands were suddenly in my hair and his mouth was on mine. I didn't know how to react. His lips were soft but demanding as he licked and bit my bottom lip. Then he pulled my top lip into his mouth and sucked gently. "I've been wanting to taste this sweet plump lip since you walked into my living room," he murmured before slipping his tongue into my mouth as I gasped at his words. He tasted like mint and something rich. My knees went weak and I reached up to grab his shoulders to hold myself steady. Then his tongue caressed mine as if asking me to join him. I took a small swipe of his mouth and then bit down gently on his lower lip. A small groan came from his throat and the next thing I knew I was being lowered onto the small bed behind me.

Rush's body came over mine and the hardness that I knew was his erection pressed between my legs. My eyes rolled back in my head and I heard a helpless moan come from my lips.

"Sweet, too sweet," Rush whispered against my lips before tearing his mouth away and jumping back off of me. His eyes zeroed in on my dress. I realized it was now up around my waist and my panties were showing. "Mother *fucking* shit," he cursed then slammed a hand against the wall before jerking the door open and exiting like he was being chased.

The wall shook from the force he put into closing it. I didn't move. I couldn't. My heart was racing and there was a familiar ache between my legs. I'd been turned on before watching sex on television but never this intensely. I was so close. He hadn't wanted to like it but he had. I'd felt that but then I'd also seen him having sex with some girl. In addition, I knew last night he'd had sex with another girl and then sent her packing. Getting Rush hard wasn't a large feat. I hadn't actually accomplished anything. He was just mad because it had been me that had turned him on.

It hurt. Knowing he disliked me so much that he didn't want to think I was attractive. The throb between my legs slowly faded as reality set in. Rush hadn't wanted to touch me. He had been furious because he had. Even turned on he had been able to walk away from me. I had a feeling I was in a minority. Most girls that wanted him got him. He couldn't bring himself to mess with me. I was the poor white trash he was stuck with until I got enough money to move out.

I rolled over and curled up into a ball. Maybe I wouldn't be wearing this dress again. It now held even more sad memories. It was time I packed it away for good. Tonight though, I'd sleep in it. This would be my farewell to a dream. The one where I was enough for some guy to want.

EIGHT

The house was once again a wreck when I woke up the next morning. This time I left the mess and hurried to work. I didn't want to be late. I needed this job now more than anything else. My dad had yet to call to check on me and I was pretty sure Rush hadn't spoken with his mother or my father because he hadn't mentioned it. I didn't want to ask him because I didn't want his anger at my father to be directed at me.

There was already a good chance that Rush would be asking me to leave when I got back to his house today. He hadn't seemed real happy with me when he'd stormed out of my room last night. And I'd kissed him back and sucked on his lip. Oh God, what had I been thinking? I hadn't been thinking. That was the problem. Rush had smelled too good and tasted too good. I hadn't been able to control myself. Now, there was a good chance I would find my bags on the porch when I got home. At least, I had money to stay in a motel.

Dressed in my shorts and polo I made my way up the office steps to the front door. I needed to clock in and get a key to the beverage cart.

Darla was already inside. I was beginning to think she lived here. She was here when I left and when I arrived every day. Her small whirlwind personality was scary though. You almost wanted to salute her when she barked orders at you. She was frowning up at a girl I hadn't seen before. She was pointing her finger and almost yelling.

"You can't consort with the members. That is the first rule. You signed the papers Bethann; you know the rules. Mister Woods came in here early this morning letting me know that his father wasn't happy with this turn of events. I only have three cart girls. If I can't trust you to stop sleeping with the members then I have to let you go. This is your last warning. Do you understand me?"

The girl nodded. "Yes, Aunt Darla. I'm sorry," she murmured. Her long dark hair was pulled back in a ponytail and her baby blue polo showcased a very large chest. Then there were her long tanned legs and round butt. And she was Darla's niece. Interesting.

Darla's angry gaze shifted to mine and she let out a relieved sigh. "Oh good, Blaire you're here. Maybe you can do something with this niece of mine. She's on probation because she can't seem to stop screwing the members while she's on the clock. We aren't a brothel. We are a country club. I'm going to have her ride with you for the next week and you are to watch her closely. She's going to learn from you. Mister Woods sings your praises. He is very pleased with the job you're doing and asked me to allow you to work in the dining room at least two days a week. I'm now looking for another cart girl, so I can't afford to fire Bethann." She said her niece's name with a growl and glared back at her.

The girl hung her head in shame. I felt sorry for her. I was terrified of upsetting Darla. I couldn't imagine being yelled at like that.

"Yes, ma'am," I replied as she held out the cart keys for me. I took them and waited for Bethann to move toward me.

"Go on with her now, girl. Don't stand here and pout. I should call your daddy and tell him what you're doing but I don't have it in my to break my brother's heart. So go out there and get some morals." Darla pointed to the door and I didn't wait around any longer. I hurried out the door and down the steps. I'd go get the drink cart ready and wait on Bethann there.

"Hey, wait up," the girl called from behind me. I stopped and looked back at her as she ran to catch up. "Sorry, that was brutal in there. I wish you hadn't seen or heard it."

She was . . . nice. "That's okay," I replied.

"I go by Bethy by the way. Not Bethann. That's just what my dad calls me so my Aunt Darla does too. And you're the infamous Blaire Wynn I've heard so much about." The smile in her voice told me she wasn't being mean.

"I'm sorry if your aunt has shoved me down your throat." I

cut my eyes over at her and her bright red plump lips curved into a smile.

"Oh, I wasn't talking about my aunt. I was talking about the guys. Woods especially likes you a lot. I hear that you caused a little stir last night at that bitch Nan's birthday party. Wish I could have seen that but the hired help doesn't get invites to those things."

I loaded the cart while Bethy stood there watching me. She was twirling a lock of her long brown hair around her finger and smiling at me. "So, you're my only in. Tell me all about it."

There wasn't much to tell. I shrugged and walked over to get into the driver's side once I had the cart loaded. "I went to the party because I'm sleeping under the stairs at Rush's until I have enough money to move out which should be real soon. It was a mistake. He didn't like me showing up. That's about it."

Bethy plopped down on the seat beside me and crossed her legs. "That is not at all what I heard. Jace said that Rush saw Woods touching you and went ape shit."

"Jace misunderstood. Trust me. Rush doesn't care who touches me."

Bethy sighed, "It sucks being the poor folks, doesn't it? The hotties never look at us seriously. We're just another fuck."

Was that really the way it was for her? Had she just given in and become the girl they tossed aside? She was too pretty for that. Guys back home would drool at her feet. They might not have millions in the bank but they were good guys from good families.

"Aren't there any attractive guys who aren't filthy rich around? The crowd that comes here can't be all there is to choose from. Surely you can find a guy who doesn't cast you aside the next morning."

Bethy frowned and shrugged. "I don't know. I've always wanted to bag a millionaire, ya know? Live the good life. But I'm beginning to see that isn't in the cards for me."

I made my way to the first hole. "Bethy, you're beautiful. You deserve more than what you're getting. Start shopping for a man somewhere else. Find one that doesn't want you for sex. Find one that wants you. Just you."

"Well hell, I may have just fallen in love with you too," she replied teasingly and laughed. She propped her feet up on the dash as I pulled up to the first golfers of the morning.

I didn't see a younger guy anywhere. They typically weren't early morning risers. For a little while I wouldn't have to worry about keeping Bethy from doing the nasty in the bushes or wherever it was she was doing it while working.

Four hours later, when we pulled up to the third hole for the third time I recognized Woods and company. Bethy sat up straight in her seat and the excited expression on her face put me on high alert. She was like a little puppy dog waiting for someone to throw her a bone. If I didn't like her so much I wouldn't even bother helping her keep this job. Being her babysitter wasn't in my job description.

Woods frowned when we pulled up beside them. "Why are

you driving Bethy around?" he asked the moment we came to a complete stop.

"'Cause she's helping me keep from fucking your friends and pissing you off. Why'd you go and tell Aunt Darla?" she pouted, crossing her arms over her bountiful chest. I had no doubt every guy standing around us was zeroed in on those big knockers of hers.

"I didn't ask her to do that. I asked that she promote Blaire, not stick her with you," he snapped and pulled his phone from his pocket. What was he doing?

"Who are you calling?" Bethy asked in a panicked tone sitting up straight.

"Darla," he snarled.

"No wait," Bethy and I said at the exact same time.

"Don't call her. I'm fine. I like Bethy. She's good company," I assured him.

He studied me a moment but didn't hang up the phone.

"Darla, it's Woods. I've changed my mind. I want Blaire inside four days a week. You can use her on the course on Fridays and Saturdays since it is so busy and she is the best you have but the rest of the time I want her inside." He didn't wait for a response before ending the call and dropping it back into the pocket of his starched plaid shorts. On anyone else those looked ridiculous but a guy like Woods could pull them off. The white polo shirt he was wearing was also immaculately pressed. I wouldn't be surprised if it was brand new.

"Aunt Darla is gonna be mad. She has Blaire babysitting me for the next couple weeks. Who will keep me in check now?" she asked casting her sultry gaze toward Jace.

"Please man, if you like me even a little, turn your head and let me take her back to the club house for just a few minutes. Please," Jace begged as he drank in the sight of Bethy sitting there with her legs up on the dash slightly open so that her crotch was in full view. The shorts we wore were too short and tight to leave a whole lot to the imagination in a position like that.

"I don't care what the hell you do. Fuck her if you want. But if dad gets wind of it again I'll have to fire her. He's pissed about the complaints."

I knew Jace wouldn't stand up for her if she was fired. He'd let her go and move on. There was no love in his gaze only lust.

"Bethy, don't," I pleaded quietly beside her. "On my night off, you and I will go out and we'll find some place where there are guys worth your time. Just don't lose your job over him," I was talking so quietly only Bethy could hear me. The others knew I was saying something to her but they didn't know what.

Bethy turned her gaze to me and pulled her knees together. "Really? You'd go out with me and look for guys? On my turf?"

I nodded and a smile broke across her face. "Deal. We're going honky-tonking. I hope you own some boots."

"I'm from Alabama. I own boots, tight jeans and a gun," I replied with a wink.

She cackled with laughter and put her feet down. "Okay boys, what do you want to drink? We have another hole to get too," she said stepping out of the cart and walking to the back. I followed her and we handed out drinks and took money.

Jace tried to grab her butt a few times and whisper in her ear. She finally turned around and smiled at him. "I'm done being your fuck buddy. I'm going out with my girl here this weekend and we're going to find us some real men. The kind that don't have a trust fund but have calluses on their hands from good hard work. I've got a feeling they know how to make a girl feel real special."

I had to swallow the laugh that bubble up inside my chest at Jace's shocked expression. I turned on the cart as Bethy jumped back in beside me.

"Damn, that felt good. Where have you been all my life?" she asked clapping her hands as I drove off smiling and waving at Woods as we headed to the next hole.

We made it through the rest of the course then stopped to restock. No more issues. I knew we might see Woods and his friends again but I had faith in Bethy to stand firm. Bethy had chatted happily about everything from her hair color to the last pregnancy scare they'd had in town with a worker and a member.

I wasn't paying attention to the members at the first hole. I was driving and trying to concentrate on Bethy's endless chatter. Bethy's muttered "crap" caught my attention.

I glanced at her and then followed her gaze to the couple

on the first hole. Rush was instantly recognizable. The tan shorts he wore and snug pale blue polo shirt looked so out of place on him. It didn't fit with the tattoos I knew covered his back. He was a rocker's son and that bled through on him even with preppy golfers clothing on his body. He turned his head and his eyes met mine. He didn't smile. He just looked away as if he didn't know me. No acknowledgement. Nothing.

"Bitch alert," Bethy whispered. I shifted my gaze from him to the girl with him. Nanette, or Nan as he referred to her. His sister. The one he didn't like talking about. She was wearing a tiny white skirt that looked like she was ready to go play tennis. She had on a matching blue polo and a white sun visor sat atop her strawberry blonde locks.

"You aren't a fan of Nannette?" I asked already knowing the answer from her comment.

Bethy let out a short laugh. "Uh, no. And neither are you. You're enemy number one for her."

What was that supposed to mean? I couldn't ask her because we had stopped just six feet from the tee and the brother and sister combo.

I didn't try to make eye contact with Rush again. He apparently didn't want to make small talk.

"You're kidding me. Woods hired her?" Nan hissed.

"Don't," Rush replied in a warning tone. I wasn't sure if he was protecting her or me or just trying to stop a scene. Either way it annoyed me.

"Can I get y'all a drink?" I asked with the same smile I bestowed on every other member when I asked this question.

"At least she knows her place," Nan said with an amused snide tone.

"I'll take a Corona. Lime, please," Rush said.

I chanced a glance his way and his eyes met mine only briefly before he turned to Nan. "Get a drink. It's hot," he told her.

She smirked at me and placed a well-manicured hand on her hip. "Sparkling water. Wipe it off though because I hate the way it comes out all wet from the water."

Bethy reached into the cooler and got out the water. I guess she was afraid I might hurl it at Nan's head. "Haven't seen you out here lately, Nan," Bethy said, as she wiped off the bottle with the towel we were supplied for this reason.

"Probably because you're too busy in the bushes with God knows who spreading your legs instead of working," Nan replied.

I clenched my teeth and popped the top off Rush's Corona. I wanted to throw the drink in Nan's smug face.

"That's enough, Nan," Rush scolded her lightly. What was she, his damn kid? He was acting like she was five. She was an adult for crying out loud.

I handed Rush the Corona careful not to look at Nan. I was afraid I might have a moment of weakness. Instead, my eyes met his as he took the bottle.

"Thanks," he said and slipped a bill into my pocket. I didn't have time to react before he was stepping away taking Nan by the elbow. "Come on and show me how you still can't kick my ass out here," he said in a teasing tone.

Nan nudged his arm with her shoulder. "You're going down." The sincere fondness in her voice as she spoke to him surprised me. I couldn't imagine someone as mean as she appeared, to be nice to anyone.

"Let's go," Bethy hissed, grabbing my arm. I realized I'd been standing there watching them.

I nodded and started to turn when Rush glanced back over his shoulder toward me. A small smile touched his lips and then he was looking at Nan again telling her which club to use. Our moment was over. If that even was a moment.

Once we were out of earshot I looked at Bethy. "Why did you say that about me being enemy number one?"

Bethy squirmed in her seat. "Honestly, I don't know exactly. But Nan is possessive of Rush. Everyone knows that . . ." she trailed off and she wouldn't make eye contact with me. She knew something but what did she know? What was I missing?

NINE

A few cars were parked outside when I got back to Rush's after work. At least I wouldn't catch him having sex. Now that I knew how good his kisses were and how nice it felt to have his hands on me, I wasn't sure I could handle seeing him doing that to someone else. It was ridiculous. But it was true.

I opened the door and stepped inside. Sexy music was playing loudly over the sound system that was piped into every room. Well, every room but mine. I started to the kitchen when I heard a female moaning. My stomach knotted up. I tried to ignore it but my feet had firmly planted themselves on the marble floor. I couldn't move.

"Yes, Rush, baby, just like that. Harder. Suck it harder," she cried out. I was instantly jealous and that just made me mad. I shouldn't care. He had kissed me once and been so disgusted he'd cursed and taken off running.

I was moving toward the sound even thought I knew it was something I did not want to see. It was like a train wreck. I couldn't not go see it even if I didn't want it seared into my brain.

"Mmmmm yes, please touch me," she begged. I cringed but I kept moving in that direction. Stepping into the living room, I found them on the couch. Her top was completely off and one of her nipples was in his mouth as his hand played between her legs. I couldn't watch this. I needed to get out of here. Now.

Spinning around, I hurried for the front door, not caring if I was quiet or not. I'd be in my truck and out of the driveway before either of them calmed down enough to realize they'd been seen. He had been going at it right there on the couch for anyone to walk in and see. He had known I would be home any moment. The fact was, he'd wanted me to see them. He was reminding me that he was something I could never experience. Right now, I never wanted to.

I drove through town angry at myself for wasting gas. I needed to save my money. I searched for a pay phone but there wasn't one to be found anywhere. The days of payphones were long gone. If you didn't have a cellphone you were screwed. I wasn't sure who I would call anyway. I could call Cain. I hadn't spoken to him since I left last week. Normally we talked at least once a week. But without a phone we couldn't do that.

I had Grant's number tucked away in my luggage. But then why would I call him? That would be odd. I really had nothing to say to him. I pulled over into the parking lot of the one and only coffee shop in town and parked the truck. I could go drink some coffee and look at magazines for a few hours. Maybe by then Rush would be done with his fuck fest downstairs.

If he'd been trying to send me a message I had received it loud and clear. Not that I needed one. I'd already resigned myself to the fact that guys with money were not for me. I liked the idea of finding a good guy with a regular job. One that would appreciate my red dress and silver heels.

I jumped down out of my truck and started toward the coffee shop when I saw Bethy inside with Jace. They were in a heated discussion at a table in the far back corner but I could see them through the window. At least she had brought him some place public. I would hope for the best with her and leave it alone. I wasn't the girl's mother. She was more than likely older than me. At least she looked older. She could make up her own mind who she wanted to waste her time with. The salty sea air tickled my nose. I crossed the street and headed to the public beach instead. I could be alone there.

The waves crashing against the dark shore was soothing. So I walked. I remembered my mother. I even allowed myself to remember my sister; it was something I rarely did because the pain was too much at times. Tonight, I wanted that distraction. I needed to remember I'd suffered far worse than some stupid attraction to a guy that was absolutely not my type at all. I let memories of better days flood my thoughts . . . and I walked.

When I pulled the truck back into Rush's driveway it was after midnight and there were no cars outside. Whoever had been here was now gone. I closed the door to my truck and headed up the stairs. The front light was on making the house loom large and intimidating in the dark sky. Just like Rush.

The door opened before I reached it and Rush stood there filling up the entry. He was here to tell me to leave. I was expecting this anyway. I didn't even flinch. Instead, I looked around for my suitcase.

"Where have you been?" he asked in a deep husky voice.

I swung my gaze back to him. "What does it matter?"

He took a step outside the door closing the small amount of space between us. "Because I was worried."

He was worried? I let out a sigh and tucked the hair that kept blowing in my face behind my ear. "I find that real hard to believe. You were too busy with your company for the night to notice much of anything." I couldn't keep the bitterness from dripping off my tongue.

"You came in earlier than I expected. I didn't mean for you to witness that."

Like that made it better. I nodded and shifted my feet. "I came home the same time I do every night. I think you wanted me to see you. Why, I'm not sure. I'm not harboring feelings for you, Rush. I just need a place to stay for a few more days. I'll be moving out of your house and life real soon."

He muttered a curse then glared up at the sky a moment before looking back at me. "There are things about me you don't know. I'm not one of those guys you can wrap around your finger. I have baggage. Lots of it. Too much for someone like you. I expected someone so different considering I've met your father. You're nothing like him. You're everything a guy like me should stay away from. Because I'm not right for you."

I let out a hard laugh. That was the worst excuse for his behavior I'd ever heard. "Really? That's the best you've got? I never asked you for anything more than a room. I don't expect you to want me. I never did. I am aware that you and I are in two different playing fields. Your league is one I will never measure up to. I'm not the right bloodlines. I wear cheap red dresses and I have a fond connection to a pair of silver heels because my mother wore them on her wedding day. I don't need designer things. And YOU are designer, Rush."

Rush reached for my hand and pulled me inside. Without a word, he pushed me up against the wall and caged me in with both his hands pressed flat against the wall beside my head. "I'm not designer. Get that through your head. I can't touch you. I want to so damn bad it hurts like a motherfucker but I can't. I won't mess you up. You're . . . you're perfect and untouched. And in the end you would never forgive me."

My heart pounded against my chest painfully. The sorrow in his eyes wasn't something I had been able to see outside. In here I could see emotion in those silver depths. His forehead was creased as if something was hurting him.

"What if I want you to touch me? Maybe I'm not so untouched. Maybe I'm already tainted." My body was pretty much untouched but staring up into Rush's eyes I wanted to ease his ache. I didn't want him to stay away from me. I wanted to make him smile. That beautiful face shouldn't look so haunted.

He ran a finger down the side of my face and traced the curve of my ear then brushed his thumb over my chin. "I've been with a lot of girls, Blaire. Trust me, I've never met one as fucking perfect as you. The innocence in your eyes screams at me. I want to peel every inch of your clothing off and bury myself inside you, but I can't. You saw me tonight. I'm a screwed up sick bastard. I can't touch you."

I had seen him tonight. I'd seen him the other night too. He screwed lots of girls, but me he didn't want to touch. He thought I was too perfect. I was on a pedestal and he wanted to keep me there. Maybe he should. I couldn't sleep with him and not give him a piece of my heart. He was already weaseling his way in. If I let him have my body he could hurt me in a way no one had ever been able to. My guard would be down.

"Okay," I said. I wasn't going to argue. This was right. "Can we at least be friends? I don't want you to hate me. I'd like to be friends." I sounded pathetic. I was so lonely I'd stooped to begging for friends.

He closed his eyes and took a deep breath. "I'll be your friend. I'll try my damnedest to be your friend but I have to be careful. I can't get too close. You make me want things I can't have. That sweet little body of yours feels too incredible tucked underneath me," he dropped his voice and lowered his mouth to my ear, "and the way you taste. It's addictive. I dream about it. I fantasize about it. I know you'll be just as delicious in . . . other . . . places."

I leaned into him and closed my eyes as his breathing grew heavy in my ear. "We can't. Fuck me. We can't. Friends, sweet Blaire. Just friends," he whispered then pushed away from me and stalked toward the stairs. I leaned back against the wall and watched him walk away. I wasn't ready to move just yet. My body was sizzling from his words and his closeness.

"I don't want you under those damn stairs. I hate it. But I can't move you up here. I'll never be able to stay away from you. I need you safely tucked away," he said without looking back at me. His hands gripped the railing on the staircase until his knuckles turned white. He stood there one more minute before shoving himself off and running the rest of the way up the stairs. When I heard a door slam I sunk to the floor.

"Oh, Rush. How are we going to do this? I need a distraction," I whispered into the empty foyer. I needed to find someone else to focus on. Someone that wasn't Rush. Someone that was available. It was the only way I was going to keep from falling too far. Rush was dangerous to my heart. If we were going to be friends then I needed to find someone else to focus my attention on. And fast.

TEN

Darla had not been happy about my move to the dining room. She wanted me on the course. She also wanted me overseeing Bethy. According to Bethy she wasn't seeing Jace anymore. She'd met him for coffee because he'd called her twenty times that afternoon. She told him if she was going to be his dirty little secret then it was over. He'd begged and pleaded but refused to acknowledge her to his circle of friends so she dumped him. I was so proud.

Tomorrow was my day off and Bethy had already come looking for me to make sure we were still on for the honky-tonk. Of course we were. I needed a man, any man to get my thoughts off Rush.

I followed Jimmy around all day. He trained me. He was attractive, tall, charismatic and very gay. The members of the club didn't know this though. He flirted with the women shamelessly. They ate it up. He would look back at me and wink when one would whisper naughty things in his ear. The guy was a playboy and a good one at that.

Once his shift was over we headed back to the staff breakroom and hung up the long black aprons we had to wear over our uniform. "You're going to be brilliant, Blaire. The men love you and the women are impressed by you. No offense sugar, but girls with hair as platinum blonde as yours normally can't walk a straight line without giggling."

I smiled at him. "Is that so? I take offense to that comment."

Jimmy rolled his eyes and reached out to pat my head. "No, you don't. You know you're one badass blonde bombshell."

"Already making a move on the new server, Jim?" Woods' familiar voice asked. Jimmy gave him a cocky grin.

"You know better than that. I got a specific taste," he let his voice drop to a sexy whisper as he trailed his eyes down Woods' body.

I glanced back at Woods who was scowling uncomfortably and I couldn't help but laugh. Jimmy joined me. "Love making the straight boys squirm," he whispered in my ear, then slapped my butt and walked out the door.

Woods rolled his eyes and walked further into the room once Jimmy was gone. Apparently, he was aware of Jimmy's sexual preference.

"Did you enjoy your day?" he asked politely.

I had enjoyed my day. Immensely. It was a much easier job than sweating it out in the heat dealing with leering old men all day. "Yes. It was great. Thank you for making it possible for me to work in here."

Woods nodded. "You're welcome. Now, how about we go celebrate your promotion with the best Mexican food on the coast?" He was asking me out again. I should go. He would be a distraction. He wasn't exactly the working class type I was looking for but who said I was going to marry him and have his babies? An image of Rush flashed in my mind and the tortured expression he'd had last night. I couldn't bring myself to date someone he knew. If he really meant what he said then I needed to keep his world at arm's length. I didn't belong in that world.

"Can I take a rain check? I didn't sleep well last night and I'm exhausted."

Woods' face fell some but I knew he would have no problem finding someone to take my place.

"There is a party tonight at Rush's, but I guess you knew that," Woods said, watching me closely for my reaction. I didn't know about the party but then Rush never warned me about them.

"I can sleep through it. I've gotten used to them." That was a lie. I wouldn't go to sleep until the last person stomped up the stairs.

"What if I come? Could you spend a little time with me before you go to bed?"

Woods was determined. I would give him that. I started to tell him no when it dawned on me that Rush would be screwing some girl tonight. He'd take her up to his bed and make her feel things he would never allow me to feel. I did need a distraction.

He'd probably already have her in his lap by the time I got home.

"You and Rush don't seem very close. Maybe we could hang out a bit outside down by the beach? I don't know if it's a good idea for you to be in the house where he can see you."

Woods nodded. "Okay. I'm good with that. But I have one question, Blaire," he said watching me closely. I waited. "Why is that? Until the other night at his house, Rush and I have been friends. We've grown up together. The same circles. Never had an ounce of trouble. What set him off? Is there something going on between the two of you?"

How did I answer that? No because he won't allow it and it is safer for my heart if we keep it only friends?

"We're friends. He's protective."

Woods nodded slowly but I could tell he didn't believe me.

"I don't mind the competition. I just like to know what I'm up against."

He wasn't up against anything because all he and I would ever be was friends. I wasn't looking for a guy in his crowd. "I'm not and will never be part of your crowd. I don't intend to seriously date anyone that is a part of your elite circle."

I didn't wait for him to argue. Instead, I walked around him and out the door. I needed to get home before the party got too wild. I did not want to see Rush wrapped up with some girl.

It wasn't a wild ragger. It was just about twenty people. I walked past several of them on my way to the pantry. A couple of them were in the kitchen fixing drinks and I smiled at them before stepping into the pantry and then my backroom.

If his friends hadn't known I slept under the stairs, they did now. I changed out of my uniform and pulled out an ice blue sundress to slip on. My feet hurt from being on them all day so I was going barefoot. I shoved my suitcase back under the stairs and stepped into the pantry to come face to face with Rush. He was leaning against the door leading into the kitchen with his arms crossed over his chest and a frown on his face.

"Rush? What's wrong?" I asked when he didn't say anything.

"Woods is here," he replied.

"Last time I checked he was a friend of yours."

Rush shook his head and his eyes quickly scanned my body. "No. He isn't here for me. He came for someone else."

I crossed my arms under my breasts and took the same defensive pose. "Maybe he is. Do you have a problem with your friends being interested in me?"

"He isn't good enough. He's a sorry ass fucker. He shouldn't get to touch you," Rush said in a hard angry tone.

Maybe he was those things. I doubted it, but maybe he was. It didn't matter. I wasn't going to let Woods touch me. His nearness didn't make my stomach do flips and the ache between my legs start up.

"I'm not interested in Woods that way. He is my boss and possibly a friend. That's all."

Rush ran his hand over his head and the silver flat ring on his thumb caught my eye. I hadn't seen him wear it before. Who had given it to him?

"I can't sleep while people are going up and down the stairs. It keeps me up. Instead of sitting in my room alone wondering who you're upstairs screwing tonight, I thought I'd talk to Woods out on the beach. Have a conversation with someone. I need friends."

Rush flinched like I'd hit him. "I don't want you outside with Woods talking."

This was ridiculous. "Well, maybe I don't want you screwing some girl but you will."

Rush pushed off from the door and came toward me backing me into my small room until we were both inside. One more inch and I would be falling back onto my bed. "I don't want to fuck anyone tonight," he paused then smirked, "that isn't exactly true. Let me clarify, I don't want to fuck anyone outside of this room. Stay here and talk to me. I'll talk. I said we could be friends. You don't need Woods as a friend."

I put both my hands on his chest to push him back but I couldn't make myself do it once I had my hands on him. "You never talk to me. I ask the wrong question and you stalk away."

Rush shook his head. "Not now. We're friends. I'll talk and I won't leave. Just please, stay in here with me."

I looked around the small rectangle that barely had room for my bed. "There isn't a lot of room in here," I said, glancing back at him and forcing my hands to stay flat on his chest and not fist his snug fitting shirt into my hands and pull him closer.

"We can sit on the bed. We won't touch. Just talk. Like friends," he assured me.

I let out a sigh and nodded. I wasn't going to be able to turn him down. Besides, there was so much I wanted to know about him.

I sank down onto the bed against the headboard and leaned back. I crossed my legs underneath me.

"Then we'll talk." I said with a smile.

Rush sat down onto the bed and leaned back against the wall. A deep chuckle came from his chest and I watched as a real smile broke out on his face. "I can't believe I just begged a female to sit and talk to me."

In all honesty, I couldn't either.

"What are we going to talk about?" I asked, wanting him to start this. I didn't want him to feel as if this was the Spanish Inquisition. I had so many questions whirling around in my head that I knew I could overwhelm him with my curiosity.

"How about how the hell you're still a virgin at nineteen?" he said, turning his silver pools toward me.

I'd never told him I was a virgin. He had called me innocent the other night. Was it that obvious? "Who said I'm a virgin?" I asked in the most annoyed tone I could muster.

Rush smirked, "I know a virgin when I kiss one."

I didn't even want to argue about this. It would only make the fact I was a virgin all the more obvious.

"I was in love. His name is Cain. He was my first boyfriend, my first kiss, my first make-out session, however tame it may have been. He said he loved me and claimed I was the only one for him. Then my mom got sick. I no longer had time to go on dates and spend time with Cain on the weekends. He needed out. He needed freedom to get that kind of relationship from someone else. So, I let him go. After Cain, I didn't have time to date anyone else."

Rush frowned. "He didn't stick by you when your mom was sick?"

I didn't like this conversation. If someone else pointed out what I already knew it would be hard not to have angry feelings about Cain. I'd forgiven him a long time ago. I'd accepted it. I didn't need bitterness toward him to creep in now. What good would that do?

"We were young. He didn't love me. He just thought he did. Simple as that."

Rush sighed, "You're still young."

I wasn't sure I liked the tone in his voice when he said that. "I'm nineteen, Rush. I've taken care of my mother for three years and buried her without any help from my father. Trust me, I feel forty most days."

Rush reached his hand across the bed and covered mine with his. "You shouldn't have had to do that alone."

No, I shouldn't but I didn't have any other options. I loved my mom. She deserved so much more than she got. The only thing that eased the ache was reminding myself that Mom and Valerie were together now. They had each other. I didn't want to talk about my story anymore. I wanted to know something about Rush.

"Do you have a job?" I asked.

Rush chuckled and squeezed my hand but didn't let go. "Do you believe everyone must have a job once out of college?"

I shrugged. I had always thought people worked at something. He had to have some purpose. Even if he didn't need the money.

"When I graduated college I had enough money in the bank to live the rest of my life without a job, thanks to my dad." He looked over at me with those sexy eyes hooded by thick black lashes. "After a few weeks of doing nothing but partying I realized I needed a life. So I began playing around with the stock market. Turns out, I'm pretty damn good at it. Numbers were always my thing. I also donate financial support for Habitat for Humanity. A couple months out of the year I'm more hands-on and I go work on site. Summers I take off from everything that I can and come here and relax."

I hadn't been expecting that.

"The surprise on your face is a little insulting," Rush said with a teasing lilt to his voice.

"I just didn't expect that answer," I replied honestly.

Rush shrugged and moved his hand back to his side of the bed. I wanted to reach over and grab it and hold onto it but I didn't. He was done touching me.

"How old are you?" I asked.

Rush grinned, "Too old to be in this room with you and way too damn old for the thoughts I have of you."

He was in his early twenties. He had to be. He didn't look

any older. "I will remind you that I am nineteen. I'll be twenty in six months. I'm not a baby."

"No sweet Blaire, you are definitely not a baby. I'm twenty-four and jaded. My life hasn't been normal and because of it I have some serious screwed up shit. I've told you there are things you don't know. Allowing myself to touch you would be wrong."

He was only five years older than me. That wasn't so bad. He gave money to Habitat for Humanity and even did onsite labor? How bad could he be? He had a heart. He had let me live here when he had wanted nothing more than to send me packing.

"I think you underestimate yourself. What I see in you is special."

Rush pressed his lips together tightly then shook his head. "You don't see the real me. You don't know what all I've done."

"Maybe," I replied, leaning forward. "But what little I have seen isn't all bad. I am beginning to think there might just be another layer to you."

Rush lifted his eyes to meet mine. I wanted to curl up in his lap and just stare at those eyes for hours. He opened his mouth to say something then closed it . . . but not before I saw the silver in his mouth.

I pulled my knees under me and moved closer to him. "What is in your mouth?" I asked, studying his lips and waiting on him to open up again.

Rush opened his mouth and slowly stuck out his tongue. It was pierced with a silver barbell.

"Does it hurt?" I asked, studying his tongue closely. I'd never seen anyone with a pierced tongue before.

He pulled his tongue back in his mouth and grinned. "No."

I remembered the tattoos on his back from the night he'd been having sex with the girl. "What are the tattoos on your back?"

"An eagle on my lower back with his wings spread and the emblem for Slacker Demon. When I was seventeen my dad took me to a concert in L.A. and afterwards he took me to get my first tat. He wanted his band branded on my body. Every member of Slacker Demon has one in the exact same place. Right behind their left shoulder. Dad was high as a kite that night but it was still a really good memory. I didn't get a chance to spend a lot of time with him growing up. But every time I saw him he either added another tat or piercing to my body."

He had more piercings? I studied his face and then let my eyes fall to his chest. A low chuckle startled me and I realized I'd been caught looking.

"No piercings there, sweet Blaire. The others are in my ears. I put a halt to the piercings and tats when I turned nineteen."

His dad was covered in tats and piercings just like the rest of Slacker Demon. Was it something that Rush hadn't wanted to do? Had his dad forced him?

"What did I say to make you frown?" he asked, slipping a finger under my chin and tilting my head up so that I was looking at him.

I didn't want to answer this truthfully. I was enjoying our

time together. I knew if I delved too deep too soon he'd take off running. "When you kissed me last night I didn't feel the silver barbell thingy."

Rush's eyelids lowered and he leaned forward. "Because I wasn't wearing it."

He was now.

"When you, uh, kiss someone with it in can they feel it?"

Rush sucked in a sharp breath and his mouth came even closer to mine. "Blaire, tell me to leave. Please."

If he was about to kiss me then I wasn't telling him anything of the like. I wanted him here. I also wanted to kiss him with that thing in his mouth.

"You would have felt it. Everywhere I want to kiss you, you would feel it. And you would enjoy it," he whispered in my ear before pressing a kiss to my shoulder and taking a deep breath. Was he smelling me?

"Are you . . . are you going to kiss me again?" I asked breathlessly as he pressed his nose to my neck and inhaled.

"I want to. I want to so fucking bad but I'm trying to be good," he murmured against my skin.

"Could you not be good for just one kiss? Please?" I asked, scooting closer to him. I would be in his lap soon.

"Sweet Blaire, so incredibly sweet," he said, as his lips touched the curve of my neck and shoulder. If he kept this up I would start begging.

His tongue came out and took a quick swipe at the tender skin on my neck then he trailed kisses along my jawline until his mouth hovered over mine. I started to plead again but he pressed one soft kiss to my lips and it stopped me. Then he pulled back but only an inch. His warm breath still bathed my lips.

"Blaire, I'm not a romantic guy. I don't kiss and cuddle. It's all about the sex for me. You deserve someone who kisses and cuddles. Not me. I just fuck, baby. You aren't meant for someone like me. I've never denied myself something I want. But you're too sweet. This time I have to tell myself no."

As his words sunk in I whimpered from the erotic sound of those naughty words rolling off his tongue. It wasn't until he stood up and grabbed the doorknob that I realized he was going to walk away from me. Again. Leaving me like this.

"I can't talk anymore. Not tonight. Not alone in here with you." The sadness in his tone made my heart hurt a little. Then he was gone and closing the door behind him.

I leaned back against the headboard and groaned in frustration. Why had I let him in here? This hot and cold game he was playing was out of my league. I wondered where he would go now. There were plenty of females out there he would kiss. Ones he had no problem kissing if they begged.

The stomping of people going up stairs rattled above my head. I wasn't getting any sleep for a while. I didn't want to stay in here and Woods was expecting me. There was no reason to stand him up. I wasn't in the mood to talk to him but I could at least tell him that I wasn't up for a beach chat.

I walked into the kitchen. Grant's back was to me and he had some girl pressed up against the counter. Her hands were tangled in his wild brown curls. They seemed very preoccupied. I quietly exited out the backdoor hoping I didn't walk up on any other makeout sessions.

"I didn't think you were going to show," Woods' voice came from the darkness.

I turned to see him leaning against the railing watching me. I felt guilty for not coming out here first and letting him know I wasn't going to meet him. I couldn't manage to make wise decisions where Rush was involved.

"I'm sorry. I got sidetracked." I didn't want to explain.

"I saw Rush exit the little cubby hole he has you in back there," he replied.

I bit my lip and nodded. I was busted. Might as well fess up.

"He didn't stay long. Was it a friendly visit or was he kicking you out?"

It was . . . it was a nice visit. We did talk. Up until I asked him to kiss me again it had been fun. I'd enjoyed his company. "Just a friendly chat," I explained.

Woods let out a hard laugh and shook his head. "Why don't I believe that?"

Because he was smart. I shrugged.

"We still on for our walk down to the beach?"

I shook my head. "No. I'm tired. I came out here to get a breath of fresh air and hopefully find you to explain."

Woods gave me a disappointed smile and pushed away from the railing. "Well, all right then. I'm not gonna beg."

"I wouldn't expect you to," I replied.

He walked back toward the doors and I waited until he was back inside before breathing a sigh of relief. That hadn't been so bad. Maybe now he would back off some. Until I figured out what to do with this attraction I had for Rush I didn't need anyone else confusing me more.

I gave it a few minutes then turned and followed him inside. Grant was no longer at the bar with the girl. They'd gone for a more secluded spot apparently. I started toward the pantry door when Rush walked into the kitchen followed by a giggling brunette. She was hanging on his arm and acting like she couldn't walk steadily. Either it was from alcohol or the six-inch heels she was bobbling on.

"But you said," she slurred and kissed the arm that she was clinging to. Yep, she was drunk.

Rush's eyes met mine. He'd be kissing her tonight. She wouldn't even have to beg. She'd also taste like beer. Was that a turn on for him?

"I'll take off my panties down here if you will," she said, not even taking note that they weren't alone.

"Babs, I've already told you no. I'm not interested," he replied without looking away from me. He was turning her down. And he wanted me to know.

"It'll be naughty," she said loudly then burst into another fit of laughter.

"No, it will be annoying. You're drunk and your cackling is giving me a headache," he replied. His eyes still hadn't left mine.

I dropped my eyes from his and started for the door to the

pantry when Babs finally noticed me. "Hey, that girl is going to steal your food," she whispered loudly.

My face flushed. Dangit. Why did that embarrass me? I was being stupid. She was drunk off her ass. Who cared what she thought?

"She lives here; she can have whatever she wants," Rush replied.

My head snapped back up and his eyes hadn't left me.

"She lives here?" the girl asked.

Rush didn't say anything else. I frowned at him and decided the one witness we had wouldn't remember this in the morning. "Don't let him lie to you. I'm the unwelcomed guest living under his stairs. I've wanted a few things and he keeps telling me no."

I didn't wait for his response. I opened the door and stepped inside. Score one for me.

ELEVEN

I finished the last of my peanut butter sandwich and dusted off the crumbs in my lap then stood up. I was going to need to go to the grocery store and buy new food soon. Peanut butter sandwiches were getting old.

I was off work today and I wasn't sure what I was going to do. I'd lain in bed thinking about Rush and how stupid I was most of the night. What did the guy have to do to convince me he just wanted to be friends? He'd stated this more than once. I needed to stop trying to get him to see me as something more. I'd made that jab at him last night. I shouldn't have done that. He didn't want to kiss me. I couldn't believe I'd begged him to.

I opened the pantry door and stepped into the kitchen. The smell of bacon met my nose and if Rush hadn't been standing at the stove with nothing but a pair of pajama pants on then I'd have been completely wrapped up in the delicious smell. The view of Rush's bare back took away from the bacon.

He glanced over his shoulder and smiled. "Good morning. Must be your day off."

I nodded and stood there wondering what a friend would say. I didn't want to break the rules anymore with him. I was going to play by his rules. I'd be moving out soon enough anyway.

"Smells good," I replied

"Get out two plates. I make some killer bacon."

I wished I hadn't eaten the peanut butter sandwich now. "I've already eaten, but thank you."

Rush put his fork down and turned to face me. "How have you already eaten? You just woke up."

"I keep peanut butter and bread in my room. I had some before I came out."

Rush's forehead wrinkled as he studied me. "Why do you keep peanut butter and bread in your room?"

Because I don't want his endless stream of friends to eat my food. I couldn't exactly say that though. "This isn't my kitchen. I keep all my things in my room."

Rush tensed and I wondered what I'd said to make him mad. "Are you telling me that you only eat peanut butter and bread when you're here? That's it? You buy it and keep it in your room and that is all you eat?"

I nodded, unsure why this was a big deal.

Rush slammed his hand down on the counter top and turned back around to face his bacon while muttering a curse.

"Go get your stuff and move up stairs. Take any room on the left side of the hall you want. Throw that damn peanut butter away and eat whatever the hell you want in this kitchen."

I didn't move. I wasn't sure where this reaction had come from.

"If you want to stay here, Blaire, then move your ass upstairs now. Then come down here and eat something out of my *motherfucking* fridge while I watch."

He was angry. At me?

"Why do you want me to move upstairs?" I asked cautiously.

Rush dropped the last piece of bacon onto a paper towel and turned off the gas stove top before looking back at me.

"Because I want you to. I hate going to bed at night and thinking about you asleep under my stairs. Now I have the image of you eating those damn peanut butter sandwiches all alone in there and it's a little more than I can deal with."

Okay. So, he does care about me in some capacity.

I didn't argue. I went back into my room under the stairs and pulled my suitcase out from under the bed. My peanut butter was inside. I unzipped it and pulled out the almost empty jar and the bag with four slices of bread left. I'd leave this in the kitchen and then go find a room. My heart was pounding in my chest. This had become my safe place. Being upstairs took away my seclusion. I wasn't alone up there.

Stepping back out of the pantry I walked over and put the peanut butter and bread down on the counter. I headed for the hallway without making eye contact with Rush. He was standing at the bar gripping the edges tightly as if he was trying to keep from hitting something. Was he considering throwing me back into the pantry? I didn't mind staying in there.

"I don't have to move upstairs. I like that room," I explained and watched his grip only tighten more.

"You belong in one of the rooms upstairs. You don't belong under the stairs. You never did."

He wanted me upstairs. I just didn't understand his sudden change of heart.

"Would you at least tell me which room to take? I don't feel right picking one out. This isn't my house."

Rush finally let go of the death grip he had on the counter and turned his eyes to meet mine. "The rooms on the left are all guest rooms. There are three of them. I think you'll enjoy the view from the last one. It looks out over the ocean. The middle room is all white with pale pink accents. It reminds me of you. So, you go choose. Whichever one you want. Take it then come down here and eat."

He was back to wanting me to eat again.

"But I'm not hungry. I just ate—"

"If you tell me you ate that damn peanut butter again I am going to throw it through a wall." He paused and took a deep breath. "Please, Blaire. Come eat something for me."

Like any woman on the planet would be able to turn that down. I nodded and headed for the stairs. I had a room to pick out.

* * *

The first room wasn't appealing. It had dark colors and the view was on the front yard. Not to mention it was closest to the stairs and the noise level from the parties would be hard to overlook. I went to the next room and the king size bed was covered in white ruffles and pretty pink pillows. A pink chandelier hung from the ceiling. It was very sweet. Not something I expected to find in Rush's house. Then again his mother lived here most of the time.

I opened the last door on the left. There were large windows that went from the floor to the ceiling and overlooked the ocean. It was gorgeous. The pale blue and green color scheme was accented with a king size bed that looked like it was made from driftwood. At least the headboard and footboard did. It had a very coastal feel. I liked it. No, scratch that. I loved it. I put my suitcase down and walked over to the door that led into a private bathroom. Large white fluffy towels and expensive soaps decorated the white marble. Splashes of blue and green were in the room but for the most part it was white.

The tub was a large round one with jets in it. Although I'd never seen one before I knew this was a Jacuzzi. Maybe I had come into the wrong room. Surely this one wasn't a guest bedroom. I'd want this room if I lived here.

Nevertheless, it was on the left side of the hallway. It had to be one of the rooms he'd mentioned. I walked back out of the bathroom. I'd go tell him I'd picked this room and if this one was wrong he'd tell me. I left my suitcase against the wall right inside the door and then headed back downstairs.

Rush was sitting at the table with a plate of bacon and some scrambled eggs when I walked back into the kitchen. His eyes immediately lifted to meet mine.

"Did you choose a room?" he asked.

I nodded and walked over to stand on the other side of the table. "Yes. I believe so. The one you said had a great view is it . . . green and blue?"

Rush smiled. "Yes it is."

"And you're okay with me staying in that room? It is really nice. I'd want that room if this were my house."

Rush's smile widened. "You haven't seen my room yet."

His must be even nicer. "Is your room on the same floor?"

Rush picked up a piece of bacon. "No, mine takes up the entire top floor."

"You mean all those windows? That's all one big room?" The top floor looked like it was made of glass from the outside. I always wondered if it was an illusion or if it was several rooms.

Rush nodded, "Yep."

I wanted to see his room. He wasn't offering so I didn't ask.

"Did you already put your things away?" he asked, then took a bite of his bacon.

"No, I wanted to check with you before I unpacked. I should probably just keep everything in the suitcase. By the end of this next week I'll be ready to move out. My tips at the club are good and I've saved most all of it."

Rush stopped chewing and his eyes turned hard as he glared

at something outside. I followed his gaze; I saw nothing but the empty beach.

"You can stay as long as you want to, Blaire."

Since when? He'd told me I had a month. I didn't reply.

"Sit beside me and eat some of this bacon." He pulled out the chair beside his and I sat down without arguing. The bacon did smell good and I was ready for something other than peanut butter.

Rush moved his plate over to me. "Eat."

I picked up a piece of bacon and took a bite. It was crispy and greasy just the way I liked it. I finished the piece off and Rush nudged the plate at me again. "Eat another."

I fought back a giggle at his sudden need to feed me. What was wrong with him? I took another piece of bacon and ate it enjoying the taste.

"What are your plans for today?" Rush asked once I swallowed.

I shrugged. "I don't know yet. I thought I'd look for an apartment maybe."

Rush's jaw ticked and his body tensed up again. "Stop talking about moving out, okay? I don't want you moving until our parents get home. You need to talk to your dad before you run off and start living alone. It isn't exactly safe. You're too young."

This time I did laugh. He was being ridiculous. "I am not too young. What is it with you and my age? I am nineteen. I'm a big girl. I can live on my own safely. Besides, I can hit a moving target better than most police officers. My skills with a gun are pretty impressive. Stop with the unsafe and too young thing."

Rush cocked an eyebrow. "So you really do have a gun?"

I nodded.

"I thought Grant was just being funny. His sense of humor sucks sometimes."

"Nope. I pulled it on him when he surprised me my first night here."

Rush chuckled and leaned back in his chair crossing his arms over his broad chest. I forced myself to keep my eyes at his face and not look down.

"I'd have loved to have seen that."

I didn't respond. It had been a bad night for me. Rehashing it wasn't something I was up for today.

"I don't want you to stay here just because you're young. I get that you can take care of yourself or you at least think you can. I want you here because . . . I like having you here. Don't leave. Wait until your dad gets back. It sounds like you two are way overdue for a visit. Then you can decide what you want to do. For now, how about you go upstairs and unpack? Think of all the money you can save living here. When you do move out then you'll have a nice padded bank account."

He wanted me here. The silly smile that tugged at my lips couldn't be helped. I'd stay and he was right, I could save money. Once Dad got back I'd talk to him and then move. There was no reason to go if Rush wanted me here.

"Okay. If you really mean that then thank you."

Rush nodded and leaned forward to put his elbows on the table. His silver stare was leveled on me. "I mean it. But that also means that the friend thing with us needs to remain in full effect."

He was right, of course. Us living together and getting involved in any way would be difficult. Besides, once this summer was over he'd move off to another house somewhere. I didn't need that kind of heartache.

"Agreed," I replied. His shoulders didn't ease and his body remained strung tight.

"Also, you are going to start eating the food in this house when you're here."

I shook my head. No I wasn't. I was not a mooch.

"Blaire, this isn't up for argument. I mean it. Eat my damn food."

I pushed my chair back and stood up. "No. I will buy food and eat it. I am not . . . I'm not like my father."

Rush muttered something and he pushed back his chair and stood up. "You think I don't know that by now? You've been sleeping in a damn broom closet without complaint. You clean up after me. You don't eat properly. I am aware that you're nothing like your dad. But you *are* a guest in my home and I want you eating in my kitchen and treating like it's yours."

This was going to be an issue. "I'll put my food in your kitchen and eat it in here. Will that be better?"

"If all you intend to buy is peanut butter and bread then no. I want you eating properly."

I started to shake my head when he reached out and grabbed my hands in his.

"Blaire, it will make me happy to know you're eating. Henrietta buys the groceries once a week and stocks this place expecting me to have a lot of company. There is more than enough. Please. Eat. My. Food."

I bit my bottom lip to keep from laughing at his pleading look.

"Are you laughing at me?" he asked with a small grin tugging at his lips.

"Yeah. A little," I admitted.

"Does this mean you're gonna eat my food?"

I sighed, "Only if you let me pay you weekly."

He started to shake his head no and I pulled my hands from his and started to walk away.

"Where are you going?" he asked from behind me.

"I'm done arguing with you. I will eat your food if I pay for my part. That's the only deal I will agree to. So take it or leave it."

Rush growled, "Okay fine. Pay me."

I glanced back at him. "I'm going to go unpack. Then take a bath in that big ole tub and then I don't know. I don't have plans until tonight."

A frown puckered his brow. "With who?"

"Bethy," I replied.

"Bethy? The cart girl who Jace messes around with?"

"Correction. The cart girl that Jace used to mess around

with. She wised up and is moving on. Tonight we're going honky-tonking to pick us up some hard working blue collar men."

I didn't wait for him to respond. I hurried to the stairs and ran up them. Once I reached my new room, I closed my door behind me and sighed in relief.

TWELVE

I might not have the clothes for Rush's parties but I had everything I needed to go to a honky-tonk. It had been awhile since I'd worn my blue jean skirt. It was shorter than I remembered but it worked. Especially with my boots.

Rush had left this morning while I was taking my bath and he hadn't been back since. I wondered if my room was off limits to his friends if he had a party here. I didn't like the idea of strangers having sex on my bed. I didn't really like the idea of anyone but me having sex on the bed I was supposed to sleep in. I wanted to ask but I wasn't sure how to go about asking something like that.

Leaving before Rush got back meant I wouldn't know what to expect. Should I plan to wash my bedding when I got home? The idea made me cringe. When my foot hit the bottom step the front door swung open and Rush walked inside. When his eyes found me he froze and slowly took in my appearance. I wasn't dressed to impress his crowd but there was a crowd out there that I might get some attention from.

"Day-um," he muttered and closed the door behind him.

I didn't move. I was trying to figure out how to approach the strangers having sex on my bed thing.

"You, uh, wearing that out to go clubbing?" he asked.

"It's called honky-tonking. I'm pretty sure it's a completely different thing," I corrected him.

Rush ran his hand over his short hair and let out a sigh that sounded somewhat frustrated and somewhat amused. If he was about to start making cracks about my clothing I might throw my boot at him.

"Can I come with y'all tonight? I've never been honky-tonking."

What? Did I just hear him correctly?

"You want to go with us?" I asked in confusion.

Rush nodded and his eyes trailed down my body once again. "Yeah, I do."

I guess he could go too. If we were friends then we should be able to hang out together.

"Okay. If you really want to. We need to leave in ten minutes though. Bethy is expecting me to pick her up."

"I can be ready in five," he said and took the stairs two at a time as he ran up them.

That was completely not what I had expected. Strange turn of events.

* * *

Seven minutes later, Rush was back down the stairs and dressed in a pair of snug jeans and a tight black tee shirt that had Slacker Demon written on the front in a white gothic print. The emblem that was on his shoulder also graced the tee shirt. The silver thumb ring was once again on his hand and for the first time since I'd met him he had a couple of small hoop earrings in his ear. He looked more like the son of a world famous rock star than he ever had. His black lashes made it permanently appear as if he were wearing eyeliner and that only added to the effect.

When my eyes made their way back up to his face he stuck out his tongue to flash his silver barbell at me and then winked. "I figure if I'm going to a honky-tonk with guys in boots and cowboy hats I needed to stay true to my roots. Rock and Roll is in my blood. I can't pretend to fit in anywhere else."

I laughed as he smirked at me. "You're going to look as out of place tonight as I do at your parties. This should be fun. Come on, rock star spawn," I teased and headed for the door.

Rush opened the door and stood back so I could walk outside. The guy could be so strange when he wanted to. "Since your friend is riding with us, why don't we take one of my cars instead? We'd all be more comfortable than in your truck."

I stopped and glanced back at him. "But we'd fit in better if we took my truck."

Rush pulled out a small remote and one of the doors on his four car garage opened up. A black Range Rover with metallic rims and a perfectly shiny paint job sat in the spotlight. I couldn't disagree with him. We'd be much more comfortable in that vehicle.

"That's certainly impressive," I replied.

"Does that mean we can take mine? I'm not crazy about sharing a seat with Bethy. The girl likes to touch things without permission," Rush said.

I smiled, "Yes, she does. She's a bit of a flirt, isn't she?"

Rush cocked an eyebrow. "Flirt is a kind word for her."

"Okay. Sure. We can take the badass Rush Finlay's killer wheels if he insists."

Rush shot me a cocky grin and headed toward the garage. I followed close behind.

He opened my door for me, which was sweet but made this feel more like a date. I didn't need him messing with my head. I was firmly set that we were just friends. He needed to play the game right. "Do you open all your friend's car doors?" I asked, standing there looking at him. I wanted him to see the error of his very polite ways.

His easy smile disappeared and a serious expression took its place. "No," he replied, stepping back to head for the driver's door. I felt like a complete jerk. I should have just said thank you and overlooked it. Why did I have to be the one to remind him of his own rules?

Once we were inside the Range Rover Rush cranked it up and pulled out without a word. I hated the silence. I'd made it awkward. "I'm sorry. I didn't mean to sound rude."

Rush let out a sigh and his shoulders eased. Then he shook his head. "No. You're right. I just don't have any female friends so I'm not good at balancing what I should do and what I shouldn't."

"So, you open doors for your dates? That's a very chivalrous thing to do. Your mother raised you right."

I felt a twinge of jealousy. There were girls out there that got that kind of treatment from Rush. Ones that he wanted to take out and be more than friends with.

"Actually, no I don't. I . . . you . . . you just seem like the kind of girl who deserves to have her door opened. It just made sense in my head at the moment. But I get what you're saying. If we're going to be friends I need to draw a line and stay behind it."

My heart melted a little more.

"Thank you for opening it for me. It was sweet."

Rush shrugged and didn't say anything else.

"We need to pick Bethy up at the club. She'll be at the office behind the clubhouse at the golf course. She had to work today. She's showering and dressing there."

Rush turned toward the country club. "How did you and Bethy become friends?"

"We worked together one day. I think we were both in need of a friend. She's fun and free spirited. Everything I'm not."

Rush let out a laugh. "You say that like it's a bad thing. You don't want to be like Bethy. Trust me."

He was right. I didn't want to be like Bethy but she was fun to be around.

I sat quietly while Rush messed with the very expensive and complicated looking stereo system. We drove the short distance from his house to the country club. "Lips of an Angel" by Hinder began to play and it made me smile. I almost expected to hear some Slacker Demon.

When the Range Rover came to a stop outside the offices I opened my door and stepped out. Bethy wouldn't be looking for this ride. She'd be looking for my truck.

The office door swung open and she sauntered out in a pair of tiny red leather shorts, a cut off white halter-top, and white leather boots up to her knees.

"What the hell are you doing in one of Rush's rides?" she asked, all smiles.

"He's going with us. Rush wants to check out a honky-tonk too. So . . ." I trailed off and looked back at the Range Rover.

"This is seriously going to cramp your chances at picking up a man. Just saying," Bethy said, as she walked down the steps and did a quick look at my outfit. "Or not. You look hot. I mean, I knew you were gorgeous but you look really hot in that outfit. I want me some real cowgirl boots. Where'd you get those?"

Her compliment was nice. I hadn't had girlfriends in so long. When Valerie had been killed the girls we'd been close to kind of faded out of my life. It was as if they couldn't be around me without remembering. Cain had become my only friend.

"Thank you, and as for the boots, I got them for Christmas two years ago from my mom. They were hers. I had loved them since she bought them and after she got, after . . . she got sick . . . she gave them to me."

Bethy frowned, "Your mom got sick?"

I wasn't in the mood to put a damper on things tonight. I nodded and forced a bright smile. "Yeah. But that's another story. Come on, let's go find us some cowboys."

Bethy returned my smile and opened the back door on my side of the Range Rover. "I'll let you ride up front because I have a sneaky feeling that is where the driver wants you."

I didn't have time to respond before Bethy had hopped up in the Range Rover and closed the door behind her. I climbed back inside and smiled over at Rush who was watching me. "Time to go get our country on," I told him.

THIRTEEN

Bethy had given Rush directions to her favorite honky-tonk. It was forty minutes outside of Rosemary. Not exactly surprising. The only country in Rosemary was the country club and that wasn't anything close to what we were walking into.

The bar was large and completely made out of what looked like wood planks. Apparently, it was famous. Probably because there weren't many of these kind of places in this area. Bright florescent beer signs graced the walls outside and inside. Miranda Lambert's "Gun Powder and Lead" was pumping out of the stereo when we walked inside.

"They have live music in about thirty minutes. That's the best time to dance. We have plenty of time to find a good spot and drink us some tequila shots first," Bethy yelled over the noise.

I had never had tequila shots. I hadn't even had beer. Tonight that would change. I was going to be free. Enjoy the night.

Rush moved in behind me and his hand settled on my lower back. This was not a friendly position . . . was it?

I decided against correcting him in here since I'd have to yell over the music. Rush led us over to an empty booth that was further back from the dance floor. He stood back and let me slide in. Bethy slid in across from me and Rush sat down beside me.

Bethy shot him a frown.

"What do you want to drink?" Rush asked, leaning down to my ear so he wouldn't have to yell.

"I'm not sure," I replied, looking at Bethy for guidance. "What do I drink?"

Bethy's eyes went wide and then she laughed. "You haven't been drinking before?"

I shook my head. "I'm not old enough to buy my own alcohol. Are you?" She clapped her hands. "This is gonna be so much fun. And yes, I'm twenty-one or at least my ID says I am." She cut her eyes to Rush. "You need to let her out. I'm taking her to the bar."

Rush didn't budge. He looked back at me, "You've never had alcohol?"

"Nope. But I intend to remedy that tonight," I assured him.

"Then you need to go slow. You won't have a very high tolerance." He reached out and grabbed a waitress' arm. "We need a menu."

Bethy put her hands on her hips. "Why are you ordering food? We're here to drink and dance with cowboys. Not eat."

Rush turned his head toward her so I couldn't see his face but I could tell his shoulders had gotten stiff. "She's never drunk before. She needs to eat first or she'll be bent over puking her guts out and cursing you in two hours time."

Oh. I didn't like to throw up. Not at all.

Bethy rolled her eyes and waved her hand in front of her face as if Rush was an idiot. "Whatever, daddy Rush. I'm going to get me somethin' to drink and I'm getting her something too. So feed her fast."

The waitress was back with a menu before Bethy was done talking. Rush took it and turned back to me opening it up. "Pick something. No matter what diva the drunk says you need to eat first."

I nodded. I didn't want to get sick.

"The cheesy fries look good."

Rush held up the menu and the waitress came running back.

"Cheesy fries. Two orders and a tall glass of water."

Once the waitress nodded and walked off, Rush leaned back and tilted his head to look over at me. "So you're at a honky-tonk. Was it everything you hoped it would be? Because I'll be real honest, this music is painful."

Smiling, I shrugged and looked around. There were guys in cowboy hats and then those that just had on regular clothes. Some had large belt buckles but for the most part they looked like people in my hometown.

"I just got here and I haven't drunk or danced yet, so I'll let you know after that happens."

Rush smirked, "You want to dance?"

I did want to dance but not with Rush. I knew how easily I'd forget that he was just a friend. "Yes, I do. But I need a shot of courage first and I need someone to ask me to dance."

"I thought I just asked," he replied.

I put my elbows on the table and rested my chin on my hand. "You think that's a good idea?" I wanted him to admit this wasn't a good idea.

Rush sighed, "Probably not."

I nodded.

Two plates of cheesy fries slid in front of us and a frozen mug with ice water was set down in front of Rush. The food looked surprisingly good. I hadn't realized I was so hungry. I needed to keep up with how much I was spending. This was seven dollars. I wasn't going to spend more than twenty dollars tonight. That might mean I only got one drink but Rush said I needed to eat so I was going to eat.

I picked up a fry smothered in cheese and took a bite.

"That's better than peanut butter sandwiches, isn't it?" Rush asked with a teasing grin. I nodded and picked up another fry.

Bethy slid in on her side of the booth carrying two drinks in small little glasses. They were yellow. "I figured I should start you out easy. Tequila is a big girl drink. You're not ready for that yet. This is a lemon drop. It's sweet and yummy."

"Eat a few more fries first," Rush interrupted her.

I took another fry and quickly ate it followed by another. Then I reached for the lemon drop. "Okay, I'm ready," I told

Bethy and she picked hers up and grinned. I watched as she put it to her lips and tilted her head back. Then I did the same.

It was really good. Only a small burn in my throat. I liked lemon. That was nice. I put the empty glass down and smiled over at Rush who was watching me.

"Eat," he replied.

I tried not to giggle at him but I couldn't help it. I laughed. He was being ridiculous.

I took another bite of my fries and Bethy reached over and got a few fries too.

"I met some guys at the bar. I pointed you out and they've been watching us since I sat down. You ready to make a new friend?"

Rush moved slightly closer to my side and the warmth from him and the warmth in my stomach made me want to stay right here by my . . . friend. Which was why I needed to get up. I nodded.

"Let her out, Rush. You can keep the booth warm for us in case we come back," Bethy said.

Rush didn't move right away and I started to think he was ignoring her or he was going to make me eat some more. He finally slid out and stood up.

I wanted to say something to him. Anything to make him smile and stop scowling but I didn't know what to say.

"Be careful. I'm here if you need me," he said in a low whisper as he stepped close to me. I just nodded. My chest tightened and I wanted to crawl back in that booth with him.

"Come on Blaire. Time to use you to get us free drinks and men. You are the hottest sidekick I've ever had. This should be fun. Just don't tell these guys you're nineteen. Tell everyone you're twenty-one."

"Okay."

Bethy pulled me over to two guys who were obviously checking us out. One was tall with long blond hair tucked behind his ears. He looked like he hadn't shaved in a few days and underneath his tight fitting flannel shirt his body seemed impressive. His eyes were on me, then on Bethy, and then back on me. He hadn't made up his mind yet.

The other guy had short dark brown hair that had some curl in it and a pair of really pretty blue eyes. The clear blue kind that makes you want to just sigh. His white tee-shirt didn't leave much to the imagination and his broad chest was nice to look at. He was as blue collar as they come. I'd know a pair of Wranglers anywhere and he wore them well. His eyes were on me. Not moving or shifting. A small smile was on his lips and I decided this wasn't going to be so bad after all.

"Boys, this is Blaire. I got her away from her brother and she now needs a drink."

The one with dark hair stood up and held out his hand, "Dalton. It's nice to meet you, Blaire."

I slipped my hand in his and shook it. "It's nice to meet you too, Dalton."

"What can I get you to drink?" he asked, a smile spreading across his face in an approving way.

"She wants a lemon drop. It's her thing," Bethy said beside me.

"Hey, Blaire, I'm Nash." The blond said, holding out his hand and I shook it. "Hello, Nash."

"Okay boys, let's not fight. There are two of us. Cool down, Nash. The innocence pouring off her has you in heat," Bethy said in an annoyed tone. "Come dance with me and I'll show you how naughty girls can satisfy that itch."

Bethy had Nash's complete attention now. I covered my mouth to keep from laughing. She was good. Bethy winked at me and led Nash out onto the dance floor.

"Some friend you got there. She was offering to take us both on. I explained I wasn't into that kind of thing and she pointed you out. All I could see was that curly blonde hair of yours and I was intrigued," Dalton said, handing me a lemon drop.

"Thank you. And yes, Bethy is a lot of fun. She brought me out tonight. This is my first time at a place like this."

Dalton nodded his head in Rush's direction. A tall leggy blonde was perched on the edge of our table. I watched as his finger ran up the side of her thigh. Sure didn't take him long.

"That why your brother came out with you tonight?"

Dalton's question reminded me why I was here and I tore my eyes off Rush and the girl's leg. "Um, uh . . . something like that."

I put the glass to my lips and drank it down quickly.

"Can we . . . I mean do you want to dance?" I asked when I put the glass back on the bar.

Dalton stood up to lead me onto the dance floor. Bethy was already pressing her body against Nash in ways that should be illegal in public. I was not going to dance like that. I hoped Dalton didn't expect it.

Dalton took my hands and put them around his neck before sliding his hands around my waist and pulling me closer to him. This was nice. Kind of. The music was slow and sexy. Not exactly something I wanted to dance to with a stranger.

"You live around here? I've never seen you in here before," Dalton said, lowering his head to my ear so I could hear him.

I shook my head. "I live about forty minutes away and I just moved there. I'm from Alabama."

He grinned. "That explains the southern twang in your voice. I knew it was thicker than any of the locals in this area."

Dalton's hand slipped further down my waist until his fingers were brushing against the top curve of my bottom. This concerned me a little.

"Are you in college?" he asked, his hand sliding an inch lower.

I shook my head, "No. I . . . uh . . . work."

I searched the crowd for Bethy and didn't see her anywhere. Where had she gone? As much as I hated to I looked over toward the booth to see if Rush was still there. The blonde was now in the booth with him. His eyes and it looked like maybe his lips were on her.

Dalton's hand slipped lower until it was cupping my butt completely. "Damn girl, your body is incredible," he murmured in my ear. Red alert. I needed help.

Wait. Since when had I needed help? I hadn't relied on anyone in years. I didn't need to start acting helpless now. I put both hands on Dalton's chest and pushed him back. "I need some air and I don't much like strange men groping my ass." I informed him and spun around to head for the exit. I did not want to go back to the booth and watch Rush make out with some girl and I sure didn't want to find another dance partner just yet. I needed fresh air.

Stepping outside into the darkness I took a deep breath and leaned up against the side of the building. Maybe I wasn't cut out for this kind of thing? Or maybe it was too much too soon. Either way I needed a breather and a new dance partner. Dalton wasn't gonna work out.

FOURTEEN

"Blaire?" Rush's concerned tone surprised me and I snapped my eyes open and strained in the darkness to see him walking over toward me.

"Yes," I replied.

"I couldn't find you. Why are you out here? This isn't safe."

I'd had it with his big brother role. I could handle things myself. He needed to back off. "I'm fine. Go back inside and continue your make-out session in our booth." The bitterness in my voice was obvious. It couldn't be helped.

"Why are you out here?" he repeated, slowly taking another step toward me.

"Because I want to be," I replied just as slowly, glaring up at him.

"The party is inside. Isn't that what you wanted? A honky-tonk with men and drinks? You're missing it out here."

"Back off, Rush."

Rush took one more step toward me leaving all but an inch between us. "No. I want to know what happened."

Something in me snapped and I put both hands on his chest and shoved as hard as I could. He barely stumbled back. "You want to know what happened? YOU happened Rush. That's what happened." I stormed around him and stalked toward the dark parking lot.

One strong hand wrapped around my arm stopping me and I jerked hard trying to set myself free but it was no use. Rush had a firm hold on me and he wasn't letting go.

"What does that mean, Blaire?" he asked, pulling me back up against his chest.

I squirmed against him fighting back the urge to scream. I hated the way the smell of him made my heart race and my body throb. I needed him to stay at a distance. Not rub his warm delicious body all over me.

"Let. Me. Go." I snapped.

"Not until you tell me what your problem is," he replied angrily.

I twisted in his arms but he didn't budge an inch. This was ridiculous. He didn't want to hear what I had to say. That realization made me want to say it. Knowing that what I was going to say would bother him. Mess up his whole friendship idea.

"I don't like seeing you touch other women. And when other men grope my ass, I hate it. I want it to be you touching me there. Wanting to touch me there. But you don't and I have to deal with it. Now, let me go!" I jerked free and ran for his Range

Rover. I could hide out there until he was ready to take me home.

Tears stung my eyes and I ran harder. When I reached his vehicle I walked around to the side and leaned back against it closing my eyes. I had just told Rush I wanted him to grope my ass. How stupid could I be? He'd given me my own room. Offered to let me stay there until my dad got home so I could save money and I'd just given him every reason to kick me out.

The locks on the Range Rover clicked and I opened my eyes to see Rush stalking toward me. He was going to take me home and kick me out. He stopped beside me and jerked open the back door. He was putting me in the back. How humiliating.

"Get in or I'll put you in," he growled.

I scrambled into the backseat before he could throw me in. But he didn't slam the door behind me. Instead, he climbed in after me.

"What are you doing?" I asked, just before he pressed me against the seat and covered my mouth with his. I opened to him with one probe from his tongue. The flick of metal in my mouth was exciting. Tonight his minty taste wasn't mixed with something else. I could taste him for hours and never get bored.

Both of his hands found my hips and he shifted me until one leg was up on the seat with my knee bent and my other one still on the floor. He'd spread me open and then settled between me. His mouth left mine and trailed hungry kisses down my neck. He took a small nip of my bare shoulder causing excitement to course through me.

Both his hands found the hem of my shirt. "Take it off," he said, as he lifted it over my head and then threw it in the front seat without taking his eyes off my chest. "I want it all off, sweet Blaire." He reached behind me with one hand and had my bra unsnapped in less than a second. He pulled it down my arms before throwing it in the front seat with my shirt.

"This is why I tried to stay away. This, Blaire. I won't be able to stop this. Not now." He lowered his head and pulled a nipple into his mouth. He sucked on it hard and an explosion went off between my legs. I cried out, grabbing his shoulders and holding on.

I watched as he stuck his tongue out and ran the metal barbell over my skin. It was the most erotic thing I'd ever seen. "Tastes like candy. Girls shouldn't taste so sweet. It's dangerous," he whispered against my skin and ran his nose along my cleavage while inhaling loudly. "And you smell incredible."

His lips were once again on mine as one of his large hands covered my breast kneading it gently and then tugging on my nipple. I wanted to feel more too. I ran my hands down his chest and slipped them underneath his shirt. I'd stared at his chest enough to know exactly what it looked like. Now I wanted to know how it felt under my hands. The warm skin that covered his hard muscles was smooth. I ran my fingers over each ripple in his stomach and memorized the feel. I had no promise that this would be more than a one-time event and I wanted it all.

Rush reached back with one arm and pulled his shirt off, tossing it aside then went back to devouring my lips with his. I arched closer to him. I'd never been topless with a guy. I wanted to feel his naked chest against mine. He seemed to know what I wanted and he wrapped me up tightly in his arms and pulled me against him. The wetness from his mouth had left my breast cold but the heat from his skin was shocking.

I cried out and pulled him closer, afraid he'd move away from me. I had what I'd wanted since I'd seen him out on the porch with that girl. It was me whose legs he was between now. This was my fantasy.

"Sweet Blaire," he whispered, pulling my bottom lip into his mouth and sucking on it.

I shifted underneath him in an attempt to get his hardness pressed between my legs. I was throbbing and I wanted to feel his erection against me. Rush slipped his hand down to caress my knee and then ran it up the inside of my thigh. I let my leg fall open even further needing him to get closer. The ache was growing and the idea of his hand being near my needy ache made me lightheaded.

The moment his finger ran along the silk crotch of my panties I jerked and let out a whimper. "Easy. I just want to see if it's as fucking sweet down there as the rest of you," Rush said in husky voice. I tried to nod but I couldn't manage anything other than remembering to breathe. I stared into Rush's silver eyes as they took on a smoky glow. He didn't look away from me as his finger slipped inside the lace edges of my panties.

"Rush," I whispered, squeezing his shoulders and holding his gaze.

"Shhh, it's okay," he replied. I wasn't scared. He was trying to ease my fear but there wasn't any. The excitement and need were too much. I needed him to hurry. Something was building inside me and I needed to reach it. The clawing ache was growing.

Rush buried his head in my neck and let out a long heavy sigh. "This is too fucking much," he groaned. I started to open my mouth and beg him not to stop. I needed him. I needed that release I knew was coming.

His finger slid over my wetness and my toes curled as my body buckled uncontrollably. Then his finger slid inside. Slowly. I froze, afraid of what this would feel like. The thickness of his finger eased in further and I wanted to grab his hand and push it in harder. This was good. Too good.

"Shit. Mother *fucking* hell. Wet, hot . . . so fucking hot. And Jesus you're so tight." Rush's breathing had gotten heavier against my neck as he said things to me that only excited me more. The naughtier his words were the more my body responded.

"Rush. Please," I begged, fighting the urge to grab his hand and force him to bring me relief from the throbbing underneath his touch. "I need . . ." I didn't know what I needed. I just needed.

Rush lifted his head and ran his nose up my neck then pressed a kiss to my chin. "I know what you need. I'm just not sure I can handle watching you get it. You've got me all kinds of worked up, girl. I'm trying hard to be a good boy. I can't lose control in the back of a damn car."

I shook my head. He couldn't stop. I didn't want him to be good. I wanted him inside me. Now. "Please, don't be good. Please," I begged.

Rush let out a rugged breath, "Shit, baby. Stop it. I'm going to explode. I'll give you your release but when I finally bury myself inside you for the first time you won't be sprawled in the back of my car. You'll be in my bed."

His hand moved before I could respond and my eyes rolled back in my head. "That's it. Come for me, sweet Blaire. Come on my hand and let me feel it. I want to watch you." His words sent me spiraling over the edge of the cliff I'd been trying so hard to reach.

"RUUUUUUSH!" I heard the loud cry that came from me as I went falling into complete bliss. I knew I was crying for him, screaming out his name and maybe even clawing at him but I could no longer control myself. The ecstasy was too much.

"Ahhhh, yeah. That's it. Fuck yes. You're so beautiful." Rush's words washed over me but they felt so far away. I was limp and gasping for air when my senses came back to me.

I forced my eyelids back so I could see if I'd mauled Rush in my wild reaction to what I knew was my very first orgasm. I'd heard enough about them but I'd never been able to make myself have one. I'd sure tried a few times but I didn't have the imagination for it. After tonight, I had a feeling that issue would no longer be a problem. Rush had just given me enough material to work with and he still had his jeans on.

I looked up at Rush who was staring down at me with his

finger in his mouth. It took a moment to register exactly what that finger was. The shocked gasp following my realization only made Rush chuckle as he pulled it out of his mouth and grinned. "I was right. You're just as sweet in that hot little pussy of yours as you are everywhere else."

If I wasn't so spent I'd have blushed. All I could do was close my eyes back tightly. Rush laughed louder. "Oh come on, sweet Blaire. You just came wild and sexy all over my hand and even left some claw marks on my back to prove it. Don't go getting shy on me now. 'Cause baby, before the night is over you will be naked in my bed."

I peered up at him, hoping I'd just heard him correctly. I wanted more of this. Much more.

"Let me get you dressed then I'll go find Bethy and see if she needs a ride or if she found a cowboy to take her home."

I stretched and then managed a nod. "Okay."

"If I wasn't hard as a damn rock right now I'd consider staying right here and enjoying the sleepy little pleased look in your eyes. I like knowing I put it there. But I need some more."

FIFTEEN

Rush wasn't lying when he said he wanted to dress me. He put my bra back on me and then pressed a small kiss to my shoulder before slipping my shirt over my head.

"I'd prefer you stay out here while I go find Bethy. You have that well pleased look on your face and it's seriously sexy. I don't want to end up in a fight."

More compliments. I wasn't sure I'd ever get used to this from him.

"I came here with Bethy because I was trying to encourage her not to sleep around with guys who would never look at her for more than a fun time. Then you came with us and now here I am in the backseat of your car. I feel like I owe her an explanation."

Rush didn't reply right away. He studied me a moment but I couldn't really read his facial expression in the darkness. "I'm trying to decide if you meant that to sound like you were doing what you encouraged her not to do." Rush moved his body back over mine and slipped his hand into my hair. "Because I've had a taste and I'm not sharing. This isn't just for fun. I may be slightly addicted."

My heart slammed against my ribs and I took a deep breath. Wow. Okay. Oh my. I managed a nod and Rush lowered his head and pressed a small kiss to my lips before running the tip of his tongue along my bottom lip. "Mmmmm, yeah. You stay here. I'll get Bethy to come out here and talk to you."

Again, all I could do was nod.

Rush moved away from me and was out of the door and sauntering back toward the honky-tonk before I could catch my breath.

He might think he was addicted but he had no idea how he made me feel. At least he could walk. I'd have never been able to stand on my own two feet so soon.

Sitting up straight, I pulled my skirt back down and scooted over by the door. I needed to get out and move to the front but I still wasn't sure I trusted my legs. Was this even normal? Should a guy be able to make you feel this way? Maybe there was something wrong with me. I shouldn't be reacting to Rush this way . . . should I?

This was one of those times I really needed a female friend. The only one I had was Bethy and I was pretty sure she wasn't the best person to give advice when it came to guys. I needed my mom.

The ache that set in when I remembered her returned and I closed my eyes to fight it off. I couldn't let that sadness in right now.

The door opened and there stood Bethy smiling at me. "Well, look at you. Making it with the hottest thing in Rosemary in the back of his Range Rover. And here I thought you wanted a blue collar man." Her words were somewhat slurred.

"Climb on in, Bethy, before you fall on your ass out here," Rush said from behind her. I looked over her shoulder. He looked annoyed.

"I don't wanna leave. I liked Earl, or was his name Kevin? No wait, what happened to Nash? I lost him . . . I think," Bethy rambled on as she climbed into the back seat.

"Who are Earl and Kevin?" I asked, as she gripped the headrest and then fell backwards onto the seat.

"Earl is married. He said he wasn't but he is. I could tell. The married ones always have the smell about 'em."

What was she talking about?

Bethy's door closed and I started to ask her more when the door beside me opened. I turned to see Rush standing there with his hand held out for me to take. "Don't try to make sense of anything she says. I found her at the bar finishing up a round of six tequila shots that married Earl had bought her. She's trashed."

This wasn't exactly how I had hoped tonight would go. I'd thought downhome country boys would be different. Maybe treat her with respect. But then she was wearing red leather short shorts. I slipped my hand into Rush's and he squeezed mine. "No need in explaining anything to her tonight. She won't remember it in the morning."

He was probably right. I stepped out of the Range Rover and he pulled me against his chest before closing the door behind me. "I want a taste of those sweet lips but I'm going to deny myself. We need to get her home before she gets sick," Rush said in a low husky whisper.

I nodded. I wanted him to kiss me too but if Bethy was going to be sick then we needed to get her home. I started to move away from him but his arms tightened around me.

"But what I said earlier. I meant it. I want you in my bed tonight."

Again, all I could do was nod. I wanted in his bed too. I might be as stupid as Bethy when it came to men after all. Rush led me over to the passenger's side and opened my door for me. "Fuck the friend thing," he muttered, grabbing my waist to help me up.

Grinning, I watched him walk back around the front of the Range Rover and climb in. "What's the grin for?" he asked once he was behind the wheel.

I shrugged. "'Fuck the friend thing.' It made me laugh."

Rush chuckled and shook his head before cranking up the Range Rover and pulling out of the now packed parking lot.

"I know something you don't know. Yes I do. Yes I do," Bethy began chanting in a sing-song voice.

I turned back to look at her. She wasn't smiling but a clumsy frown was plastered on her face. "I know something," she whispered loudly.

"I heard that," I replied and glanced over at Rush who didn't appear to be amused. He wasn't a fan of drunken Bethy.

"It's a big secret. A huge one . . . and I know it. I'm not supposed to but I do. I know something you don't know. You don't know. You don't know," Bethy started singing again.

I started to ask her what it was she knew but Rush spoke up first. "That's enough Bethy." Rush's warning was clear. I even shivered from the steeliness in his voice.

Bethy clamped her lips together and acted as if she was twisting a key and then throwing it away.

I turned back around wondering if she did know something I needed to know. Rush sure acted like she did. He'd looked ready to stop the car and toss her out.

Rush began messing with the radio for some music so I decided to remain quiet. Rush was upset because Bethy knew something she wasn't supposed to know.

He had so many secrets surrounding him. There were things he refused to talk about. We were attracted to each other. That didn't mean he had to tell me all his secrets. Did it? No! Of course not. But once again, was I ready to give a part of myself to someone I didn't really know? He was so guarded. Would I be able to do this with him and not become attached? I wasn't sure.

Rush's hand slipped over mine. I glanced over at him. He was watching the road but he was thinking. I wished I could just ask him. But we weren't there yet. We might never be. Should I give my virginity to a guy who would be walking out of my life soon with no hope of anything more?

"That was the best time, ever. I like blue-collar fellas. They're so much fun," Bethy slurred sleepily from the backseat. "You should have looked around some more Blaire. It would have been smarter on your part. Rush is a bad idea. 'Cause there is always Nan."

Nan? I turned to look back at Bethy. Her eyes were closed and her mouth was hanging open. A soft snore escaped and I knew any explanation to that comment wouldn't be happening tonight. At least not from Bethy.

I turned to look back at Rush whose hand had left mine and was now gripping the steering wheel tightly. His jaw was also clenched. What was the deal with his sister? She was his sister, right?

"Is Nan your sister?" I asked, watching him for any reaction. He simply nodded but said nothing more. This was what I'd gotten the last time I brought her up. He completely closed down on me.

"What did Bethy mean then? How would us sleeping together affect Nan?"

Rush's entire body was strung tight. He didn't respond. My heart sank. That secret, whatever it was, would keep us from doing anything more. It was too important to him therefore, it was a warning flag for me. If he couldn't tell me something even Bethy knew then we had a problem.

"Nan is my younger sister. I won't . . . I can't talk about her with you." The way he said "you" made my stomach turn. Something was off here. I wanted to ask more questions but the sadness and loss that washed over me as I realized I wouldn't be sleeping in his bed tonight or any other night stopped me. This would keep me from getting too close to Rush. I should have never let him touch me like he did earlier. Not when he could so easily toss me aside.

We remained silent all the way to the offices. Rush got out of the Range Rover without a word and woke Bethy up. Then helped her inside. It was locked but Bethy had a key. She had mumbled something about staying the night here or her daddy would kill her. I didn't go help. I didn't have the energy. I just wanted to go to bed. I wanted my bed under the stairs. Not the big new one waiting on me.

When Rush got back into the car he was still silent. I tried to figure out why he would shut down like he did over Nan and what Bethy's comment could mean but nothing made sense. It was only minutes later that we were pulling into the four car garage. I opened my door and climbed down as soon as he put it in park. I didn't wait for him as I made my way to the door. It was locked so I had to wait on him to come unlock it.

SIXTEEN

Rush opened the door and stood back so I could enter. I walked inside and headed for the kitchen.

"Your room is upstairs now," Rush said, breaking the silence.

I knew that. My mind was just elsewhere. I turned and headed for the steps. Rush didn't follow me. I wanted to look back and see what he was doing but I couldn't.

"I tried to stay away from you." His words sounded dark. I stopped and turned back around to look down at him. He was standing on the bottom step staring up at me. The pained expression on his face made my heart ache.

"That first night I tried to get rid of you. Not because I disliked you." He let out a hard bitter laugh. "But because I knew. I *knew* you'd get under my skin. I knew I wouldn't be able to stay away. Maybe I hated you a little bit then because of the weakness you'd be able to find in me."

“What is so wrong with you being attracted to me?” I asked, needing him to at least answer me that.

“Because you don’t know everything and I can’t tell you. I can’t tell you Nan’s secrets. They’re hers. I love her, Blaire. I’ve loved her and protected her all my life. She’s my little sister. It’s what I do. Even though I want you like I’ve never wanted anything in my life, I can’t tell you Nan’s secrets.”

Every word from his mouth sounded like it was being ripped from him. Nan was truly his sister and I understood that kind of loyalty and love. I would have died for Valerie if I could. She had been only fifteen minutes younger than me but I’d have done whatever she needed me to. No guy or other emotion could have made me betray her.

“I can understand that. It’s okay. I shouldn’t have asked. I’m sorry.” I was sorry. I’d pried into his life and his sister’s. Obviously whatever Bethy knew she shouldn’t know it. If Bethy thought that Rush’s need to protect his sister would be an issue for us she was wrong.

Rush closed his eyes tightly and muttered something. He was dealing with something. Maybe this had brought up a bad memory. As much as I’d like to go down there and hug him I knew I wasn’t welcomed right now. I’d messed that up.

“Good night, Rush,” I said and walked up the stairs. I didn’t look back this time. I went directly to my room.

There was no mistaking morning time up here with these windows. An alarm clock wouldn’t be needed. The sun had woken me up an hour before my alarm clock had gone off. I showered and dressed with ease now that I had a bathroom right here and more room to move around.

I wasn't in the mood to eat Rush's food this morning. I wasn't really in the mood to eat but I had two shifts to work today so I needed some food. I would stop by the coffee house and get some caffeine and a muffin. The short black linen skirt and white cotton button down top we had to wear as a uniform when we served in the dining room at the club was our responsibility to keep washed and pressed. I'd spent a few hours yesterday ironing the few I had here at home.

Once I had on my tennis shoes, I headed down the stairs. I hadn't heard any activity upstairs yet today so I knew Rush wasn't awake. For once, I was grateful to not have to face him. Now that I'd had time to sleep on last night's events I was embarrassed.

Not only had I let Rush touch me in places I'd never had anyone touch me before, but then I'd turned around and acted like a crazy nosy bitch. I needed to apologize to him but I wasn't ready to do that just yet.

I quietly closed the front door behind me and headed out to my truck. At least I wouldn't be home until after dark tonight. No having to face Rush for at least twelve more hours.

Jimmy was already in the staff room with his apron on when I arrived. He flashed me a grin and then made a pouty face with his lips. "Uh, oh, looks like someone had a bad morning."

I couldn't tell Jimmy my problems. He knew these people

too. I had to keep this stuff to myself. "I didn't sleep that well," I replied.

Jimmy made a tsking sound. "For shame. Sleep is such a beautiful thing."

I nodded in agreement and clocked in. "Am I on my own today?" I asked.

"Of course. You had this figured out after following me around for two hours. You should breeze through this day."

I was glad someone thought so. I grabbed an order tablet and a pen and stuck them in the pocket of my black apron.

"Breakfast time," Jimmy said with a wink and pushed open the door that led into the dining room. "Oooh looks like the boss and friends are at table eight. As much as I'd love to go ogle their fine asses, they would prefer you. I'll go take the early morning tennis mommas over on table ten. They tip well."

Waiting on Woods and his friends was not something that I wanted to do this morning. But I couldn't argue with Jimmy. He was right. He'd get better tips from the women. They loved him.

I headed over to their table. Woods eyes lifted to meet mine and he smiled. "You look much better in here," he said when I stopped in front of them.

"Thank you. It's much cooler," I replied.

"Blaire has moved on up. I may have to eat more meals here," the blond curly headed guy said. I still didn't know his name.

"This could be very good for business," Woods agreed.

"How was your night out with Bethy?" Jace asked with a

slight edge to his voice. He was holding the Bethy thing against me apparently. I didn't care. He was pond scum as far as I was concerned.

"We had a good time. What can I get y'all to drink?" I asked, changing the subject.

"Coffee, please," the blond chimed in.

"Okay, I get it. Off-limits. Girl code and all that shit. I want some OJ," Jace replied.

"Coffee for me too," Woods replied.

"I'll be right back with your drinks," I replied and spun around to see two more tables with guests. Jimmy was helping one of the tables so I headed for the other. It took me a second to realize just who was at that table. My feet stopped moving as I watched Nan flick her long strawberry blonde hair over her shoulder and then level a scowl at me. I glanced back over to Jimmy who was finishing up drink orders at his second table. I had to do this. I was being silly. She was Rush's sister.

I forced my feet to move and walked over to her table. She was sitting with another girl. One I hadn't seen before. She was equally as glamorous as Nan.

"Webster must be letting anyone work here these days. I need to tell Woods to speak with his daddy about being more selective with their employees," Nan drawled slowly in a rather loud voice.

My face felt warm and I knew I was red faced. Right now I just needed to prove that I could get through this. Nan hated me for unknown reasons. Unless of course, Rush had told her I was snooping into her business. It didn't sound like something Rush would do but did I know him that well. No.

"Good morning, what can I get y'all to drink?" I said as politely as possible.

The other girl snickered and ducked her head. Nan glared up at me as if I were something repugnant. "You can get us nothing. I expect a classier server when I come to eat here. You won't do."

I looked for Jimmy once again but he was gone. Nan might be Rush's little sister but she was a major bitch. If I didn't need this job so badly I'd tell her to kiss my ass and I'd walk out.

"Is there a problem here?" Woods' voice came from behind me. For once in my life, I was relieved by his presence.

"Yes, there is. You hired white trash. Get rid of her. I pay too much to be a member here to tolerate this kind of service."

Was it because I was living at her brother's house? Did she hate my dad too? I didn't want her to hate me. If she hated me, Rush would never open up to me. That door was firmly shut.

"Nannette, you've never once paid to be a member here. You're here because your brother allows it. Blaire is one of the best employees we've ever had and not one other paying member has complained. Certainly not your brother. So, pull in the claws, sweetheart, and get over yourself," Woods snapped his fingers and Jimmy came hurrying over toward us. He must have come back out during the drama and I'd missed him. "Jim, would you please serve Nan and Lola? Nan seems to have an issue with Blaire and I don't want Blaire being forced to wait on her."

Jimmy nodded. Woods took my elbow and led me back towards the kitchen. I knew we were drawing attention but I didn't care at the moment. I was just extremely grateful to be getting away from the curious onlookers and getting a breather.

Once the kitchen door closed behind me I let out the breath I'd been holding.

"I'm only going to say this once, Blaire. You stood me up the other night at Rush's. I didn't have to ask you why. I knew why when Rush was nowhere to be found. You had made your choice and I was backing off. But what happened in there is only a small taste. The bitch has serious venom in her veins. She is bitter and angry and when the time comes to choose, Rush will choose her."

I turned and stared at Woods unsure what he meant. Woods gave me a sad smile then let go of my elbow and walked back into the dining room. Woods knew the secret too. He had to. This was going to drive me crazy. What was the big deal?

SEVENTEEN

I jerked open my truck door glad to be done with the day. My eyes went to a small black box lying on my seat with a note attached. I reached over and picked it up.

Blaire,

It's a phone. You need one. I spoke with your dad and he said to get it for you. It's from him. Talk and text are unlimited so use it as you wish.

Rush

My dad had told Rush to get me a phone? Really? I opened the box and a white iPhone complete with a durable case was tucked safely inside. I pulled it out and studied it a moment. I pressed the small round button on the bottom and the screen lit up. My dad hadn't given me a gift since the birthday before he'd left.

Before Valerie had died. He'd given us matching electric scooters and helmets.

I climbed into the truck and held my phone in my hand. Could I call my dad on this? It would be nice if he explained to me why he wasn't here. Why he'd sent me to a place where I was unwanted? Had he met Nan? Surely, he would have known that she wouldn't accept me. Besides, if she was Rush's sister then she was my stepsister. Was that why she was so mad? I had grown up with less money than her? God, she was cruel.

I tapped on contacts and saw that I only had three numbers saved in my phone. The first one was Bethy, then Darla, and then Rush. He'd put his number in here. That surprised me.

The phone started playing a Slacker Demon song I'd heard on the radio before and Rush's name flashed on the screen. He was calling me.

"Hello," I said, still not sure what to think of this.

"I see you got the phone. Do you like it?" Rush asked.

"Yes, it's really nice. But why did Dad want me to have it?" He hadn't cared much about anything else I'd needed over the years. This seemed trivial.

"Safety measure. All females need a phone. Especially ones that drive vehicles older than they are. You could break down at any moment."

"I have a gun," I reminded him.

He chuckled. "Yeah, you do, badass. But a gun can't tow your truck."

Point made.

"Are you coming home?" he asked. The way he said "home" like his house was my home too made me feel warm inside. Even if he hadn't meant it that way.

"Yes, if that's okay. I can go do something else if you need me to stay away."

"No. I want you here. I cooked."

He'd cooked? For me? "Oh. Okay. Well, I'll be there in a few minutes."

"See you soon," he said and the line went dead.

Here he went being incredibly strange again.

When I walked into the house the distinct smell of taco seasoning met my nose. I closed the door and headed for the kitchen. If this was actual homemade Mexican food then I was going to be seriously impressed.

Rush's back was to me as I entered the kitchen. He was humming along to a song I didn't recognize playing over the sound system. It was smoother and slower than what he normally listened to. A bottle of Corona was opened on the bar with a slice of lime on the rim. I'd fixed many just like that while working on the course.

"Smells good," I said. Rush glanced back over his shoulder and a slow smile spread across his face.

"It is," he replied, wiping his hands on the hand towel beside him. He picked up the Corona and handed it to me. "Here, drink up. The enchiladas are almost finished. I need to flip the quesadillas and they need a few more minutes. We should be ready to eat soon."

I put the Corona to my lips and took a small sip. Mostly for courage. This was not how I expected our next encounter to go. Rush was a puzzle that I might never figure out.

"I'm hoping you eat Mexican," he said as he pulled the enchiladas out of the oven. Rush Finlay did not look like someone who belonged in the kitchen cooking. But dang, if he wasn't sexy doing it.

"I love Mexican food," I assured him. "I will admit I'm really impressed that you can cook it."

Rush looked up at me and winked. "I got all kinds of talents that would blow your mind."

I had no doubt. I swallowed a larger gulp of the Corona.

"Easy girl. You gotta eat something too. When I said drink up I didn't mean for you to gulp it down."

I nodded and wiped off the small drop that was clinging to my bottom lip. Rush watched me intently. It made my hand shake a little.

He turned his eyes away quickly and started taking the quesadillas off the skillet. He put them on a platter full of hard and soft tacos. There were even burritos. He'd made some of everything.

"Everything else is on the table already. Grab me a Corona out of the fridge and follow me."

I quickly did as I was told and hurried after Rush. He didn't stop in the dining room. Instead, he stepped outside onto the large back porch overlooking the ocean. Two hurricane lamps stood in the middle of the table so that we could have candlelight without it blowing out.

"Sit. I'll fix your plate," he said, motioning for me to take a seat at the first seat we came to. There were only two out here.

I sat down and Rush began to dish one of everything onto my plate. Then he put the tray of food down and placed the napkin from beside my plate on my lap. His mouth was so close to my ear that his warm breath made me shiver.

"Can I get you another drink?" he whispered in my ear before standing back up.

I shook my head. I wouldn't be able to drink if he was going to do things like that. My heart was racing like crazy already. I couldn't swallow a thing like this.

Rush picked up his drink and took the seat across from me. I watched as he fixed his plate then his eyes lifted to mine. "If you hate it, don't tell me. My ego can't handle it."

I was sure nothing he made would taste bad. I grinned and picked up my fork and knife to cut off a small piece of the enchilada he'd placed on my plate. There was no way I could eat all this but I could taste some of everything.

The minute it touched my tongue it surprised me. It was as good as any I'd eaten at a Mexican restaurant. Smiling, I looked at him. "It's delicious and I can't say I'm surprised."

Rush put a forkful in his mouth and smirked. His ego could never be crushed. It might even need to be brought down a few pegs. I started to taste the other things and found myself hungrier than I'd first thought. Everything was so good I didn't want to waste anything.

After my fourth taste of everything on the plate, I knew I

had to stop. I sipped my Corona and settled back in my seat. Rush was washing down his food as well. Once he finished he set the bottle down and his eyes went serious. Uh-oh. We were about to talk about last night. I had wanted to forget last night. Especially since tonight had been so nice.

"I'm sorry about how Nan treated you today," he said with a pained sincere voice.

"How did you know about that?" I asked, suddenly feeling uncomfortable.

"Woods called me. He was warning me that Nan would be asked to leave the next time she was rude to an employee." Woods was a nice guy. He could be a little too much at times but he was a good boss. I nodded.

"She shouldn't have spoken to you that way. I've had a talk with her. She promised me it wouldn't happen again. But if it does, somewhere else, then please come tell me."

This had been an apology meal for his younger sister's bad behavior, not a mending of fences between us. I wasn't on a romantic date like my imagination had managed to concoct in my head. This was just Rush apologizing for Nan.

I pushed my chair back and picked up my plate. "Thank you. I appreciate the gesture. It was very nice of you. I assure you that I don't intend to tattle to Woods if Nan is rude to me in the future. He just happened to witness it first-hand today." I picked up my drink. "Dinner was lovely. Nice to have after a long day at work. Thank you so much." I didn't make eye contact with him. I just wanted to get away from him.

Hurrying inside, I rinsed off my plate and placed it in the dishwasher before rinsing out my bottle and putting it in the recycle container.

"Blaire," Rush said from behind me, and his body was suddenly right there caging me in. His hands were on each side of the counter and all I could do was stand there and look down at the sink in front of me. His hard warm body brushed against my back and I bit my tongue to keep from making a whimper. I would not let him see how he affected me.

"This wasn't an attempt to apologize for Nan. It was an attempt to apologize for me. I'm sorry about last night. I lay in bed all night wishing you were there with me. Wishing I hadn't pushed you away. I push people away Blaire. It's a protective mechanism for me. But I don't want to push you away."

Walking away from him and keeping him at a distance was the smart thing to do. Rush wasn't and never would be anyone's Prince Charming. I couldn't ever let myself think he was the one who would love me and cherish me. He would never be that guy for me. But my heart had grown a little attached to him. It didn't mean forever but for right now I wanted Rush to be my first. He wouldn't be my last. He'd just be a stop along the path of life. A stop I might never forget or get over. That was what scared me the most. Not being able to move on.

He reached up brushing my hair from the side of my neck, and then pressed a kiss to the curve of my shoulder. "Please. Forgive me. One more chance, Blaire. I want this. I want you."

Rush would be my first. It just felt right. Inside I knew he was meant to be the guy that taught me about life. Even if he broke my heart eventually. I turned in his arms and slipped my hands around his neck.

"I'll forgive you on one condition," I said, gazing up into his emotion-filled eyes that made me hope for so much more.

"Okay," he said cautiously.

"I want to be with you tonight. No more flirting. No more waiting."

The worried expression was instantly gone and replaced with a hungry gleam.

"Hell, yes," he growled and pulled me against him.

EIGHTEEN

Rush didn't start off easy. His mouth was forceful and demanding. I was glad. It was romantic. It was real. He was also wearing his tongue barbell. I hadn't noticed it earlier but I felt it. The flick of his tongue was wicked with that thing involved. I liked tasting something I knew was unattainable.

Both of his hands cupped my face. His kisses slowed and then he pulled back still holding my face in his hands. "Come with me upstairs. I want to show you my room," he flashed me a naughty smile, "and my bed."

I nodded and Rush dropped his hands from my face. He slipped one of his hands into mine and threaded our fingers then squeezed. Without a word, he led me to the stairs pulling me gently up them in his hurry to get there. Once we got to the second floor, he pressed me up against the wall and kissed me fiercely, nipping at my lips and stroking my tongue. He jerked back and took a deep breath. "One more flight of stairs," he said in a gravelly voice and pulled me toward the door at the end of the hallway. We passed my room and he paused. At first, I thought he might want to go in there instead but he didn't stop until we reached the narrow door at the end of the hall. I'd wondered if that was the staircase leading to his room. He pulled out a key to unlock it, then opened the door and motioned for me to go ahead of him.

The stairwell was hardwood like the other set but there were walls on either side as we climbed the steep steps.

Once I reached the top step, I froze. The view was breathtaking. The moonlight highlighted the ocean giving the room the most fabulous backdrop imaginable.

"This room is why I had mom buy this house. Even at ten years old I knew this room was special," Rush whispered from behind me wrapping his arms around my waist.

"It's incredible," I breathed in a hushed voice. I felt as if talking too loud would ruin the moment.

"I called my dad that day and told him I'd found a house I wanted to live in. He wired my mother the money and she bought it. She loved the location so this is the house we spent our summers in. She has a house of her own in Atlanta but she prefers it here."

He was talking about himself. His family. He was trying. My heart melted a little more. I should stop him from edging his way any more into my heart. I didn't want it to hurt when it was over and he walked away. But I wanted to know more about him.

"I'd never want to leave," I replied in all honesty.

Rush kissed my ear softly. "Ah, but you've not seen my cabin in Vale or my flat in Manhattan."

No, I hadn't and I never would. However, I could picture him in those places. I had watched enough television to know what they looked like. This winter I could see him by a roaring fire in an elaborate cabin in the mountains with snow covering the ground outside. Or relaxing in his flat overlooking Manhattan. Maybe from his windows he could see big Christmas tree they always put up every year.

Rush turned me to the right until I was facing a king size bed. It was solid black. The bed itself and the quilt that covered it. Even the pillows were black. "And that's my bed," he said, walking me toward it with his hands on my hips. I would not think about all the girls who had been here before me. I would not. I closed my eyes and blocked that thought out completely.

"Blaire, even if all we do is kiss or just lay there and talk, I'm okay with that. I just wanted you up here. Close to me."

Another little inch or two wedged into my heart. I turned around and looked at him, "You don't mean that. I've seen you in action, Rush Finlay. You don't bring girls to your room and expect to just talk." I tried to sound teasing but my voice cracked when I mentioned the other girls.

Rush frowned, "I don't bring girls up here at all, Blaire."

What? Yes he did.

"The first night I came here you said your bed was full," I reminded him.

He smirked. "Yeah, because I was sleeping in it. I don't bring girls to my bedroom. I don't want meaningless sex tainting this space. I love it here."

"The next morning a girl was still here. You'd left her in bed and she came looking for you in her undies."

Rush slipped a hand underneath my shirt and began rubbing small circles on my back. "The first room to the right was Grant's room until our parent's divorced. I use it as my bachelor pad room now. That's where I take girls. Not here. Never here. You're my first," he paused and a grin tugged on his lips, "well, I let Henrietta come up here once a week to clean but I promise there is no hanky-panky going on between us."

Did this mean I was different? I wasn't one of many? God, I hoped so. No . . . no I didn't. I had to get a grip. He would be leaving me soon. Our worlds did not converge. They didn't even come close to each other.

"Kiss me, please," I said, standing on my tiptoes and pressing my mouth against his before he could protest or suggest we talk again. I didn't want to talk. If we talked I'd want more.

Rush pushed me back onto his bed and covered my body with his while his tongue tangled with mine. His hands ran down the sides of my body until he found my knees. He pulled my legs apart and settled in between the space he'd created.

I wanted to feel more of him. I grabbed handfuls of his shirt and tugged. He got the hint and broke our kiss long enough to pull it off and toss it aside. This time I had room to explore him. I ran my hands down his arms and the hard bulges of his biceps. I moved my hands to his chest and ran my fingers over his abs sighing in pleasure at the feel of each hard ripple. Sliding my hands up, I ran my thumb over each of his hard pecs and felt his nipples tighten under my touch. Oh my, that was sexy.

Rush pulled back and started unbuttoning the white shirt on my uniform almost frantically. When he got to the last button he pushed it back and tugged my bra down until both breasts sprang free of the lacy cups covering them.

He stuck his tongue out and flicked at one of my nipples. He moved to the other one and did the same before he lowered his head and pulled it into his mouth with one hard tug.

My body bucked against his and the hardness I'd felt brushing against my leg was now firmly wedged between my legs pressing directly on my ache. "AH!" I cried out, rubbing against his hardness and needing to feel more of it.

Rush let my nipple pop free of his mouth as he kept his eyes on me and lowered his body, leaving me once again without the pressure I needed. His hands unsnapped my skirt and he began pulling it slowly down along with my panties. He never took his eyes off me.

I lifted to allow him to pull them down over my hips with ease. Rush sat back on his knees and crooked his finger for me to sit up. I was ready to do whatever he asked. As soon as I was sitting he took my shirt the rest of the way off. Then he had my bra undone and tossed aside.

"You naked in my bed is even more unbelievably beautiful

than I thought it would be . . . and trust me I've thought about it. A lot."

He moved back over me hooking his arms under my knees and settling back down between my legs. But he still had his shorts on. I wanted those off . . . OH!

Rush moved his hips over my spread open legs and pressed right where I needed him too.

"Yes! Please!" I scratched at him needing him to come closer.

Rush lowered his body moving his hands to hold the inside of each of my thighs as he kissed my belly button and then the top of my mound. He needed more hair. I wanted to pull at something.

His silver eyes lifted and locked with mine as his tongue slipped out and he ran the metal piercing right over my clit. I screamed his name and grabbed handfuls of the sheets to keep myself on the bed. I felt like I could sky rocket out the larger than life windows.

"God, you're sweet," Rush panted as he lowered his head to put his tongue on me again. I'd heard of this. I knew about it but I never imagined it could feel this good.

"Rush, please," I whimpered.

He paused over me. The warmth of his breath bathed the throb he had created. "Please, what, baby. Tell me what it is you want."

I shook my head back and forth and squeezed my eyes tightly. I couldn't tell him. I didn't know how to say it.

"I wanna hear you say it, Blaire," Rush said in a strangled whisper.

"Please lick me again," I choked out.

"*Damn*," Rush cursed before running his tongue back through my folds. Then he pulled my swollen clit into his mouth and sent me spiraling off into space. The world erupted in color and my breathing stopped while pleasure coursed through me.

It wasn't until the descent down from my high that I realized Rush had left me and was now stripped down and lowering himself back over me.

"Condom is on; I need to be inside," Rush whispered against my ear as he pulled my legs open with his hands and I felt the tip of his shaft penetrate me.

"Holyfuck, you're so wet. It's gonna be hard not to slip right in. I'm going to try to go slow. I promise." His voice was strained and the veins in his neck stood out as he pressed further into me. It was stretching me but it felt good. The pain I had expected wasn't there. I shifted my body opening my legs further and Rush swallowed hard and froze.

"Don't move. Please baby, don't move," Rush pleaded, holding himself very still. Then he pushed further into my tightness before the pain hit. I tensed and so did Rush. "That's it. I'm gonna do it fast but then I'll stop once I'm in and let you get used to me."

I nodded and closed my eyes and reached up to grab a hold of his arms. Rush pulled back and then his hips moved forward with one hard thrust. Hot pain sliced through me and I cried out, squeezing his arms tightly and holding on while the wave of pain rocked through my body.

I could hear Rush's fast hard breathing as he held himself very still. I didn't know exactly how this felt for a guy but I could tell it wasn't easy. Rush was in some sort of pain.

"Okay. I'm okay," I whispered as the pain eased.

Rush opened his eyes and looked down at me. His eyes were smoky. "Are you sure? 'Cause baby, I want to move so damn bad."

I nodded and continued to hold onto his arms in case the pain came back when he moved. Rush's hips moved back and it felt like he was leaving me then he thrust forward slowly and filled me up again. There was no pain this time. I just felt stretched and full.

"Does it hurt?" Rush asked as he held himself still once again.

"No. I like it," I assured him.

Rush moved his hips back again and then plunged forward causing me to moan from pleasure. It felt good. More than good.

"You like that?" Rush asked in amazement.

"Yes. It feels so good."

Rush closed his eyes and threw his head back and let out a groan as he began to move faster. I could feel my body climbing higher again. Was that possible? Could I have another orgasm so soon?

All I knew was, I wanted more. I lifted my hips to meet his thrust and that seemed to make him frantic.

"Yeah. God, you're incredible. So tight. Blaire, you're so fucking tight," he said through pants as he moved inside me.

I pulled my knees up so I could wrap my legs around his waist and he began to tremble. "Are you close, baby?" he asked in a strained voice.

" I think," I replied, feeling the building inside of me. I wasn't there yet though. The pain had slowed down any pleasure in the beginning. Rush slipped his hand down between us until his thumb rubbed against my throb.

"AH! Yes, right there," I cried out and clung to him as the wave crashed over me. Rush let out a roar and went rigid and very still then he pumped into me one last time.

NINETEEN

Rush's heavy breathing in my ear as his body weighed down on mine was wonderful. I wanted to hold him here. Still inside me. Just like this.

When he moved his arms and lifted himself off me, I tightened my arms around him and he chuckled. "I'll be back. I need to take care of you first," he said and then kissed me on the lips before leaving me alone on his bed.

I watched his naked butt in all its perfection walk across the room and into what appeared to be the bathroom. I heard water running and then he was walking back out completely bare in the front. My eyes immediately went south. I heard Rush chuckle and I closed my eyes embarrassed to be caught looking.

"Don't get shy on me now," he teased then reached to reopen my knees. "Open up for me," he said softly and pulled my knees open. I noticed the washcloth in his hands for the first time.

"Not too much," he said, washing between my legs as I watched him in fascination. "Does it hurt?" he asked with concern in his voice as he gently wiped the tender area. I shook my head. Now that we weren't wild with passion this was embarrassing. But having him clean me up was sweet. Was this what guys did after sex? I'd never seen this in a movie.

Rush seemed pleased with his clean up job and he threw the used wash cloth in the trash can beside his bed. He crawled back on the bed beside me and pulled me against him.

"I thought you weren't a cuddler, Rush," I said, as he ran his nose along my neck and inhaled loudly.

"I wasn't. Only with you Blaire. You're my exception," he whispered then tucked my head under his chin and pulled the covers up over us. Sleep came fast. I was safe and I was happy.

Slow kisses being placed on the inside of my calf and along the arch of my foot was the first thing that registered with me. I forced my eyes open. Rush was on his knees at the end of the bed kissing my feet and up the side of my leg with a wicked grin on his face.

"There's your eyes. I was beginning to wonder just how much I was going to need to kiss in order to wake you up. Not that I mind kissing higher but that would lead to some more incredible sex and you now only have twenty minutes to get to work."

Work. Oh crap. I sat up and Rush put my leg down. "You've got time. I'll go fix you something to eat while you get ready," he assured me.

"Thank you, but you don't have to. I'll grab something in the staff break room when I get there."

I was trying not to let the morning after awkwardness set in. I had had sex with this man. Really good sex or at least I thought it was. Now it was daylight and I was naked in his bed.

"I want you to eat here. Please."

He wanted me here. My heart thumped harder in my chest. "Okay. I need to go to my room and get a shower."

Rush glanced back at his bathroom then at me. "I'm torn, because I want you to shower in there but I don't think I'll be able to walk away knowing you're naked and soapy in my shower. I'll want to join you."

Holding the sheet over my chest, I sat up and smiled up at him. "As appealing as that sounds I'd be late for work."

Rush sighed and nodded. "Right. You need to go to your room."

I looked around for my clothes but I didn't see them anywhere.

"Put this on. Henrietta comes today. I'll have her wash and press your clothes from last night." He threw the tee shirt he'd had on last night at me. I caught a whiff of him as it landed on my chest. I was going to have a hard time giving this back. I modestly tried to pull it over me without letting the sheet fall.

"Now stand up. I want to see you," he murmured, backing up. He was wearing a pair of pajama pants as he eased off the edge of the bed and waited for me to stand up. I let the sheet fall and I stood up. His shirt hit me just above the knees.

"Can you call in sick?" he asked as his eyes traveled down my body.

A warm tingly sensation ran through me. "I'm not sick," I replied.

"Are you sure? Because I think I have a fever," he said stepping around the bed and pulling me up against him. "Last night was amazing," he said into my hair.

I hadn't expected this kind of reaction from him. I'd been worried that he might toss me out this morning. But he didn't. He was being sweet. And so incredibly yummy I was tempted to call in sick.

It was my day on the drink cart and if I didn't show up then Bethy would have to do the whole course by herself on a Friday. That would be cruel. I couldn't.

"I have to work today. They're expecting me," I explained.

He nodded and stepped back, "I know. Run Blaire. Run your cute little ass down stairs and get ready. I can't promise you I will let you go if you stand here looking like that much longer."

Giggling, I ran past him and down the stairs. The amused laughter I left behind was perfect. Rush was perfect.

The heat was only getting worse. I really wished Darla would let me wear my hair up. I was ready to take a bottle of that ice water and pour it over my head. I'd dry in seconds out here in this heat. Why were men golfing in this weather? Were they crazy?

Pulling the drink cart to back to the first hole I noticed the dark head of hair that belonged to Woods. Great. Not who I was in the mood for today. Jace was probably wanting to wait on Bethy to make her rounds anyway. I could probably skip them. Woods turned and looked back at me and a smile touched his lips.

"Back on the cart today. As much as I like having you inside, this makes golfing a helluva lot more fun," Woods said in a teasing tone as I pulled the cart up beside them.

I wasn't going to encourage his flirting. But he was my boss so I couldn't make him mad either.

"Back off, Woods. That's a little too close," Rush's voice came from behind me and I spun around to see him walking toward us with a pair of dark blue shorts and a white polo shirt. Was he playing golf?

"So she's why you suddenly wanted to play with us today?" Woods asked.

I didn't look away from Rush as he walked toward me. He was here for me. At least I was pretty sure he was. He'd asked me where I was working today during breakfast.

His hand slipped around my waist. He pulled me up against his side and bent his head to whisper in my ear, "Are you sore?"

He'd been worried about me being sore today and having to work on my feet all day. I'd told him I was fine. I just felt stretched. Apparently he was still concerned.

"I'm fine," I replied quietly.

He pressed a kiss to my ear. "Do you feel stretched? Can you tell I've been inside you?"

I nodded, feeling my knees go a little weak from the tone in his voice.

"Good. I like knowing you can feel where I've been," he said, then pulled away from me and leveled his eyes on Woods.

"I figured this was gonna happen," Woods said in an annoyed tone.

"Nan know it yet?" Jace asked. Blondie hit him in the arm and scowled at him.

Why did Nan always come up? Would I ever know?

"This isn't Nan's business. Or yours," Rush replied, glaring at Jace.

"I came here to golf. Let's not talk about this out here. Blaire, why don't you get everyone's drinks and head on to the next hole," Woods said.

Rush tensed beside me. Woods was testing us. He wanted to see if I was going to act differently now that Rush was making some claim on me publicly. I was here to work. Just because I had slept with Rush didn't change my place in the grand scheme of things. I knew that.

I stepped out of Rush's arms to open the cooler and started handing out everyone's choice of drinks. My tips weren't as high as they used to be with this group. Except, of course, for Woods. I figured that would change today too.

I could see the hundred dollar bill that Woods put in my hands and I was sure Rush did too. I quickly closed my hand

and shoved it into my pocket. I'd deal with him later when Rush wasn't watching. Rush walked up and stuck his payment in my pocket. He kissed me softly and then winked at me before he walked over to get a golf club from the caddy.

I didn't give Woods a reason to correct me. I quickly got back on the cart and headed for the next hole. The phone in my pocket buzzed startling me. Rush had tucked it in my pocket before I left this morning. I was having a hard time remembering I had it.

I stopped the cart and pulled it out.

Rush: I'm sorry about Woods.

Why was he sorry? He had no reason to be sorry.

Me: I'm fine. Woods is my boss. No big deal.

I slipped the phone back into my pocket and headed to my next stop.

TWENTY

A driveway full of cars was not something I expected when I pulled into Rush's after work. The golf course had gotten so busy that I'd only stopped to give them drinks one more time on the sixteenth hole. He hadn't texted me again all day. My stomach knotted up nervously. Was this it? Had his brief moment of sweetness after taking my virginity faded away so soon?

I had to park out on the edge of the road. Closing my truck door, I started the trek to the door.

"You don't want to go in there," Grant's familiar voice said in the darkness. I looked around and saw a small orange glow fall to the ground then get put out under a boot before Grant stepped out of his hiding spot.

"Do you come to these parties to hang around outside?" I asked, since this was the second time I'd arrived at a party here to find Grant outside alone.

"I can't seem to quit smoking. Rush thinks I've stopped. So I hide out here when I need a smoke," he explained.

"Smoking will kill you," I told him, remembering all the smokers that I'd watched slowly dying when I took my mother to chemo treatments.

"That's what they tell me," he replied with a sigh.

I looked back at the house and heard the music pouring out of it. "I didn't know there was a party tonight," I said, hoping the disappointment in my voice didn't come through.

Grant laughed and leaned a hip against a Volvo. "Isn't there always a party here?"

No, there wasn't. After last night I thought Rush would have called me or texted me. "I guess I just wasn't expecting it."

"I don't think Rush was either. This is a Nan party. She sprung it on him. The girl has always managed to get away with murder where Rush is concerned. I got my ass kicked by Rush more than once growing up because I didn't fall for her wounded puppy shit."

I walked over to lean against the Volvo beside him and crossed my arms. "So you grew up with Nan, too?" I needed something. Any kind of explanation.

Grant cut his eyes at me. "Yeah. Of course. Georgianna is her momma. Only parent she's got. Well . . ." Grant pushed off from the Volvo and shook his head. "Nope. You almost had me. I can't tell you shit, Blaire. Honestly, when someone does, I don't want to be anywhere around."

Grant stalked back toward the house.

I watched him until he was back inside before I made my way to the house. I prayed no one was in my room. If they were I was going to the pantry. I was not in the mood for Nan. Or the secrets surrounding Nan that everyone but me was allowed to know. I sure wasn't in the mood for Rush.

I opened the door and was glad that no one was standing around to see me arrive. I headed straight for the stairs. Laughter and voices filled the house. I didn't fit in with them. There was no use in going down there and acting like I did.

I glanced at the door leading to Rush's stairs and let last night's memories wash over me. I was beginning to think that was a one-time thing. I opened my door and stepped in before I turned on the light.

I covered my mouth from the scream that bubbled up when I realized I wasn't alone. It was Rush. He was sitting on my bed looking out the window. He stood up when I closed the door and walked over to me.

"Hey," he said in a soft voice.

"Hey," I replied, unsure as to why he was in my room when he had a house full of people. "What are you doing in here?"

He gave me a crooked smile. "Waiting on you. I kinda thought that was obvious."

Smiling, I ducked my head. His eyes could be too much sometimes. "I can see that. But you have guests."

"Not my guests. Trust me, I wanted an empty house," he said, cupping the side of my face with his hand. "Come upstairs with me. Please."

He didn't have to beg. I'd go gladly. I dropped my purse on the bed and tucked my hand in his. "Lead the way."

Rush squeezed my hand and we headed up the stairs together.

Once we reached the top step Rush pulled me into his arms and kissed me hard. Maybe I was easy but I didn't care. I'd missed him today. I wrapped my arms around his neck and kissed him back with all the emotion churning inside me that I didn't quite understand.

When he broke the kiss we were both breathless. "Talk. We are going to talk first. I want to see you smile and laugh. I want to know what your favorite show was when you were a kid and who made you cry at school and what boy band you hung posters of on your wall. Then I want you naked in my bed again."

Smiling at his strange, but adorable, way of telling me he wanted to do more than just have sex with me, I walked over to the large tan sectional sofa that overlooked the ocean instead of a television.

"Thirsty?" Rush asked, walking over to a stainless steel refrigerator I hadn't taken the time to notice last night. A small bar sat off to the side of it.

"Just some ice water would be nice," I replied.

Rush went to work fixing drinks and I turned to look out at the ocean. "*Rugrats* was my favorite show, Ken Norris made me cry at least once a week but then he'd make Valerie cry and I'd get mad and hurt him. My favorite and most successful attack was a swift kick to the balls. And shamefully, *The Backstreet Boys* covered my walls."

Rush stopped beside me and handed me a tall glass of ice water. I could see the indecision on his face. He sat down beside me. "Who is Valerie?"

I'd mentioned my sister without thinking. I was comfortable with Rush. I wanted him to know me. Maybe if I opened up about my secrets he would share his. Even if he couldn't share Nan's.

"Valerie was my twin sister. She died in a car accident five years ago. My dad was driving. Two weeks later, he walked out of our lives and never returned. Mom said we had to forgive him because he couldn't live with the fact he'd been driving the car that killed Valerie. I always wanted to believe her. Even when he didn't come to Mom's funeral I wanted to believe he just couldn't face it. So I forgave him. I didn't hate him or let bitterness and hate control me. But I came here and well . . . you know. I guess Mom was wrong."

Rush leaned forward and set his glass on the rustic wooden table beside the couch and slipped his arm behind me. "I had no idea you had a twin sister," he said almost reverently.

"We were identical. You couldn't tell us apart. We had a lot of fun with that at school and with boys. Only Cain could tell us apart."

Rush began to play with a lock of my hair as we sat there looking out over the water. "How long did your parents know each other before they married?" he asked. Not a question I was expecting.

"It was a love at first sight kind of thing. Mom was visiting a friend of hers in Atlanta. Dad had recently broken up with her friend and he came around one night when Mom was at her friend's apartment alone. Her friend was a little wild from what my mom said. Dad took one look at mom and he was sunk. I can't blame him. My mom was gorgeous. She had my color hair but she had the biggest green eyes. They were like jewels almost and she was just fun. You were happy just to be near her. Nothing ever got her down. She smiled through everything. The only time I saw her cry was when she was told about Valerie. She crumpled to the floor and wailed that day. It would have frightened me if I hadn't felt the same way. It was like part of my soul had been ripped out." I stopped. My eyes were burning. I'd let myself get carried away with opening up. I hadn't opened up to anyone in years.

Rush rested his forehead on the top of my head. "I'm so sorry, Blaire. I had no idea."

For the first time since Valerie had left me I felt like someone was there I could talk to. I didn't have to hold back. I turned in his arms and found his lips with mine. I needed this closeness. I'd remembered the pain and now I needed him to make it go away. He was so good at making everything but him fade away.

"I love them. I will always love them but I'm okay now. They're together. They have each other," I told him when I felt his reluctance to kiss me back.

"Who do you have?" he asked in a tortured voice.

"I have me. I found out three years ago when my mom got

sick that as long as I held onto me and didn't forget who I was that I'd always be okay," I replied.

Rush closed his eyes and took a deep breath. When he opened his eyes the desperate look in them startled me. "I need you. Right now. Let me love you right here, please."

I pulled my shirt off and then reached for his. He lifted his arms for me as I pulled his shirt over his head. He made quick work of my bra and it was gone with nothing between us. His hands cupped my breasts as he brushed his thumb over each hard crest. "You are so fucking unbelievably gorgeous. Inside and out," he whispered. "As much as I don't deserve it I want to be buried inside you. I can't wait. I just need to get as close to you as I can get."

I scooted back from him and stood up. After slipping off my shoes, I unsnapped my shorts and pushed them down along with my panties then stepped out of them. He sat there watching me like I was the most fascinating thing he had ever seen. It felt powerful. The embarrassment I expected to feel from standing naked in front of him wasn't there.

"Get naked," I said, looking down at his erection pressing against his jeans.

I thought that would get an amused chuckle from him but it didn't. He stood up, quickly stepping out of his jeans and then sank back down on the couch pulling me with him.

"Straddle me," he instructed. I did as I was told. "Now," he gulped, "ease down on me." I looked down and saw him holding the base of his cock. I grabbed onto his shoulders and slowly lowered myself as he handled everything else.

"Easy, baby. Slow and easy. You're gonna be sore."

I nodded and bit my bottom lip as the tip started to enter me. He moved the head back and forth over my opening, teasing me. I squeezed his shoulders and gasped. It felt good. So very good.

"That's it. You're getting so fucking wet. God, I want to taste it," he growled.

Seeing the animalistic look in his eyes flipped a switch in me. I wanted to make him remember me. Remember this. I knew our time was limited and I knew I'd never forget him. Still, I wanted to know that when he walked away he'd never forget me. I didn't want to be that one girl whose virginity he took.

Leaning forward, I waited until he rubbed the head against my entrance. Then I sank down hard with a loud cry as it filled me.

"*SHIT,*" Rush shouted. I didn't wait for him to worry about me. I was going to ride him. I understood the terminology now. I was in control of this. He started to open his mouth and say something but I stopped him by plunging my tongue into his mouth while I lifted my hips and sank back down onto him again harder. The groan and buckling sensation of his body under me assured me I was doing something right.

I broke apart so I could cry out as I began riding him faster and harder. The tenderness inside me was screaming out with the stretching of his entrance but it was a good pain.

"Blaire, oh holy fuck, Blaire," he ground out as his hands

grabbed my hips and he let himself break free and enjoy the ride. His hands began taking over. He lifted me and slammed me back down onto him with fast and hard thrusts. Every curse and loud moan that escaped him made me wilder. I needed this with him.

The orgasm was building and I knew after a few more thrusts I was going to break apart on top of him. I wanted him to come too. I began rocking on him and letting out the loud cries I had been trying to control. "I'm gonna come," I moaned as the sensation built.

"Fuck baby, so good," he growled and then we both fell over the top together. His body bucked underneath me and then stilled. My name tore from his lips at the same time my body reached its climax.

When the tremors slowed and I could breathe again I wrapped my arms around his neck and collapsed on top of him.

Both his arms held me tightly to him as his breathing slowed. I liked the sweet sex we'd had last night but there was something to be said for fucking. I smiled to myself at the thought and turned my head to kiss his neck.

"Never. Never in all my life," he panted, running his hand down my back and cupping my bottom with a gentle squeeze. "That was. God, Blaire, I don't have words."

Smiling into his neck I knew I'd made my mark on this perfect, wounded, mysterious and confusing man.

"I believe the word you are looking for is epic," I said laughing as I leaned back so that I could look at him.

The tenderness in his eyes melted my heart a little more. "The most epic sex ever known to man," he replied and reached out to tuck hair behind my ears. "I'm ruined. You know that right? You've ruined me."

I wiggled my hips and I could feel him still inside me. "Hmmm no, I think you might still work."

"God, woman you're gonna have me hard and ready again. I need to clean you up."

I traced his bottom lip with the pad of my finger. "I won't bleed again. I did that already."

Rush pulled my finger into his mouth and sucked on it gently before letting it go. "I wasn't wearing a condom. I'm clean, though. I always wear a condom and I get checked regularly."

I wasn't sure how to process this. I hadn't been thinking about a condom.

"I'm sorry. You got naked and my brain kind of checked out. I promise you I'm clean."

I shook my head. "No, it's okay. I believe you. I didn't think about it either."

Rush pulled me back against him. "Good because that was fucking unbelievable. I've never felt it without a condom. Knowing I was in you and feeling you bare makes me real damn happy. You felt amazing. All hot and wet and so very tight."

I rocked against him. His dirty words in my ear made my ache wake back up. "Mmm," I replied as I felt him grow hard again inside me.

"Are you on any birth control?"

I never had a reason to be. I shook my head.

He groaned and moved my hips off him until he was out of me. "We can't do that again until you are. But you've got me all hard again." He reached between my legs and ran a finger against my swollen clit. "So sexy," he murmured. I let my head fall back and enjoyed his soft touch.

"Blaire, come take a shower with me," he asked in a strained voice.

"Okay," I said, looking back at him. He helped me up and then led me to his bigger than life bathroom.

"I want you in the shower. What we did out there was the best fucking I've ever had in my life. But in here it's gonna be slower. I'm taking care of you."

TWENTY-ONE

Leaving Rush in bed this morning had been hard. He'd been sleeping so peacefully I hadn't wanted to wake him up. I'd refrained from kissing his face before I left. Asleep he seemed so worry free. I didn't realize how intense and on guard he was until I'd watched him sleep and seen him completely at peace.

Opening the door to the staffroom I was greeted to the smell of fresh donuts and a smiling Jimmy.

"Good morning sunshine," he said cheerily as always.

"That remains to be seen . . . are you gonna share those donuts or not?"

He held the box out to me. "I bought two extras just for you doll. I knew my blonde bombshell was coming to work today and I didn't want to be empty handed."

I sat down across from him and reached for my donut. "If I thought you'd enjoy it I'd kiss your face," I teased.

Jimmy wiggled his eyebrows, "Who knows, baby? A face like yours can lead a man astray."

Laughing, I took a bite of the fluffy warm goodness. This wasn't healthy but it was so dang good.

"Eat up because we got us a long ass day ahead. The debutante ball is tonight and we won't be in the dining room. We'll all be sent to the ballroom and forced to walk around with trays of food and then serve them all at a sit down dinner."

Debutante ball? What the heck was that? "Is that why there are so many trucks outside with flowers and decorations?"

Jimmy nodded and reached for another chocolate covered donut. "Yep. Happens every year during this week. Crazy rich mommas strut their daughters around and introduce them to society. After tonight, the girls will be considered women and treated as an adult member of the club. They can be on committees and the like. It's crazy ass bullshit is what it is. Especially since Nan turned twenty-one a few weeks back. That means she gets to be released into mother fucking adulthood."

Nan was a debutante. That was interesting. Her mother wasn't here. Did this mean she was returning? My heart sped up . . . I'd have to leave soon. Rush hadn't told me that anything had changed about my moving out. When I left would he still see me?

"Breathe, Blaire. It's just a damn ball," Jimmy said. I took a deep breath. I hadn't realized I'd started to panic. This is why I'd wanted to keep my distance. I knew this day was coming. Would my dad be home today then?

"What time does it start?" I managed to ask without a hitch in my voice.

"Seven but they will close down the dinning at five to get us ready."

I nodded and put the rest of my donut down. I couldn't finish it. Today would be a waiting game. I felt the phone in my pocket but I couldn't text Rush. I didn't want him to tell me any bad news through a text message. I'd just wait.

"Blaire, I need to see you a moment in my office," Woods' voice broke into my thoughts. My eyes shot to Jimmy's and his were wide with concern. Great. What had I done?

I stood up and turned to face Woods. He didn't look angry. He smiled at me and it gave me the courage I needed to walk toward him. He held the door open for me and I stepped out into the hall.

"Relax, Blaire. You aren't in trouble. We just need to discuss tonight."

Oh. Whew. I took a deep breath and nodded then followed him to a door at the end of the hall.

"I don't get anything glamorous. Dad believes in making me work my way to the top. Even if I'll inherit the club one day." Woods rolled his eyes while opening the office door and waved me inside. The room was as large as my bedroom at Rush's. It had two large picture windows overlooking the eighteenth hole.

Woods walked over to sit on the edge of his desk instead of behind it. I appreciated his trying not to make this very formal. That would make me nervous.

"The Debutante Ball is tonight. It is an annual event around here. We make spoiled little rich bitches into adults. It's a stupid pain in the ass that makes the club over fifty million dollars in profits with fees, donations and the like. So we can't stop the nonsense. Not that my mother would if she could. She was a debutante once upon a time and you'd think she had been crowned queen of England to hear her talk about it."

I wasn't feeling better about tonight. This explanation was making it worse.

"Nan is twenty-one now. So, she'll be a debutante. I looked over the line up and Rush will be her escort; it's traditional for the girl's father or older brother to escort her. The escort must also be a member of the club. I don't know what is going on with you and Rush but I do know that Nan hates you. I don't need drama tonight. I do however, need you. You're one of our best. Question is, can you do this without a catfight? Because Nan will do her best to push your buttons. It will be all on you to ignore it. You may be dating a member but you're the help. Doesn't change that. The member is always right. The club will have to side with Nan if a fight were to break out."

What was he expecting? This wasn't high school. We were all adults. I could ignore Nan and Rush all night if need be.

"I can do this. No problem."

Woods gave a brisk nod. "Good, because the pay is excellent and you need the experience."

"I can do it," I reassured him.

Woods stood up. "I'm trusting that you can. You can go help Jimmy with breakfast now. He is probably cursing us both."

The rest of the day flew by and I was so busy with preparations that had no time to think about Nan or my father's return. Or Rush. Now I was standing in the kitchen with every other server on staff. I was in a white and black server dress with my hair pulled up onto my head in a bun. I was beginning to get butterflies in my stomach.

This was the first time I'd have to face the differences between Rush and me. His world versus mine. They would collide tonight. I had prepared myself for any remarks Nan might make about me. I had even spoken with Jimmy about being a buffer and keeping me from having to go near Nan. I wanted to see Rush or even speak to him but I had a feeling that would be frowned on.

"Show time. Hors d'oeuvres and drinks people. You know your job. Let's go." Darla was running the show tonight backstage. I picked up my tray of martinis and headed for the line-up at the door. Everyone left quickly and we all made different paths through the crowd. Mine was a semicircle clockwise. Unless I saw Nan, then I turned counterclockwise and Jimmy went clockwise. It was a good plan. I just hoped it worked.

The first couple I walked up to didn't even acknowledge me as they chatted and took a drink from the tray. That was easy enough. I made it through several more groups. Some of the men and women I recognized from the golf course. They would always nod and smile when they noticed me but that was it.

Halfway through the room my tray was empty and I made a mental note of the stopping point. I hurried back to the kitchen for more drinks. Darla was waiting for me. She shoved a new tray of martinis at me and shooed me away.

I made it back to my spot only having to stop twice and allow someone to get a drink off the tray. Mr. Jenkins called out my name and waved. I smiled back at him. He played eighteen holes every Friday and Saturday. It amazed me that a ninety-year-old man could get around that well. He also came in for coffee black and two poached eggs Monday through Friday mornings.

As I turned back from smiling his way my eyes locked with Rush's. I had tried hard not to look for him although I knew he was here. It was Nan's big night. Rush wouldn't miss it. No reason he should. She was mean but she was his sister. It was me she detested. Not him.

His face looked pained and his small smile was forced. I smiled back at him trying really hard not to think about his weird greeting. At least he had looked my way. I hadn't known what to expect from him.

Doctor and Mrs. Wallace both greeted me and told me they missed seeing me on the golf course. I lied and told them I missed it too. Then I headed back to the kitchen for yet another tray.

Darla shoved a tray with champagne at me, "Go, go, hurry," she barked.

I walked as swiftly as I could with a tray full of champagne flutes. Once in the ballroom I started my same path again through members who were deeper in conversations and I was just a tray of drinks. I liked this better. I didn't feel on edge.

Bethy's familiar giggle caught my attention and I turned to look for her. I hadn't seen her in the kitchen earlier. I'd assumed Darla hadn't wanted her to work this function. Or Woods' dad hadn't.

Bethy wasn't dressed like us. She had on a clingy black chiffon dress and her long brown hair was piled up on her head with ringlets hanging down around her face. She turned her head, catching my eyes, and she broke into a huge grin. I watched as she hurried over to me. The stiletto heels she was wearing didn't even slow her down.

"Can you believe that I'm here as a guest?" Bethy asked, looking around us in awe and then back at me. I shook my head because I couldn't.

"When Jace came to my apartment on his knees begging last night I told him if he wanted me, he had to claim me as his girlfriend in public. He agreed and well, you get the picture. Things got real hot up in my apartment. But anyways here I am," she gushed.

Jace had manned up. Good for him. I glanced over her shoulder to see Jace watching us. I smiled at him and nodded my approval. He flashed me a crooked grin with a shrug.

"I'm glad to know he got some sense knocked into him," I replied.

Bethy squeezed my arm. "Thank you," she whispered.

She didn't have anything to thank me for but I smiled. "Go have a good time. I've got to get these all passed out before your aunt comes out here and catches me talking."

"Okay, I will. I wish you could enjoy it with me, though." Her eyes glanced over my shoulder. I knew she was looking at Rush. He was here and he was ignoring me in front of all these people. He was doing it for Nan's sake but did that make it any better?

It slowly dawned on me. I'd become Bethy.

"I need the money so I can get my own place," I told her with a forced smile. "Go mingle," I encouraged her and walked off to the next group of people.

The eyes following me sent a burning sensation up my neck. I knew Rush was watching me. I didn't have to turn and see him to confirm it. Had he just had the same realization that I had? I doubted it. He was a guy. I had become available and easy. I was also the world's greatest hypocrite. I was now guilty of what I'd scolded and pitied Bethy for.

The last champagne flute left my tray and I walked back through the crowd careful not to go near Rush or Nan. I didn't even glance their way. I had some pride left. I only had to stop three times for guests to put their empty flutes on my tray as I hurried back to the safety of the kitchen.

"Good you're back. Take this tray. We need some food out there before they all drink too much and we have a high-faluting drunken mess on our hands," Darla said, handing me a tray of things I didn't recognize. They also smelled bad. I scrunched my nose and held the tray away from me. Darla cackled with laughter.

"It's escargot, snails. They're disgusting but these people think they are a delicacy. Get over the smell and go." I felt my stomach roll. I could have done without that explanation. Escargot would have been a sufficient description.

When I reached the entrance to the ballroom I steadied myself and tried not to think about the snails I was giving people to eat, or the fact that Rush was in there acting like he didn't know me at all. After I'd spent the past two nights in his bed.

"You doing okay?" Woods asked, when I walked inside the room. He was at my elbow looking concerned.

"Yes. Except for the fact I'm giving people snails to eat," I replied. Woods chuckled, took one from my tray and popped it into his mouth.

"You should try one. They're really very good. Especially soaked in garlic and butter."

My stomach rolled again and I shook my head. Woods laughed out loud this time. "You always make things more interesting, Blaire," he said, leaning down toward my ear. "I'm sorry about Rush. Just for the record, if you'd have chosen me you wouldn't be working tonight. You'd be on my arm."

I felt my face flush. It was enough to know I was a dirty little secret but for others to realize it was humiliating. I'd wanted Rush, though. So bad. Well, I'd got my wish alright.

“I need the money. I am very close to being able to afford a place of my own,” I informed him matter of factly.

Woods gave me a brisk nod and a sympathetic smile before turning to greet an elderly guest who was passing by. I took that moment to get away. I had snails to feed people.

Jimmy caught my eye and he winked at me reassuringly. He’d taken care of Rush’s side of the room brilliantly. I hadn’t even gotten close to him. Bethy smiled brightly at me when I arrived at her group. Her smile died when she looked at the food on my tray.

“What is that?” she asked in horror.

“You don’t want to know,” I informed her, causing Jace and a guy I wasn’t familiar with to laugh.

“Probably best that you let this pass on by,” Jace told Bethy as he tucked his hand around her waist and pulled her closer to his side affectionately.

She beamed up at him and that was all the sweet romance I could take. I hurried on to the next group. The curly red hair was familiar. It took me a second to place her. The evil venom in her smile reminded me exactly where I’d seen her before. She had been after Woods at Rush’s house the night of Nan’s party. I hadn’t made a fan that night thanks to Woods.

“Isn’t this fun?” she said, turning her attention away from the couple she’d been talking to and focusing on me. “Guess Woods decided you were more suited to work for him than date him.” She giggled and shook her head causing the red curls to bounce around. "I swear, this makes my night." She reached up and tipped my tray.

Snails ran down the front of my shirt followed by the tray clattering loudly on the floor. I was too stunned to move or speak.

"Oh and look, she's super clumsy. Woods should be pickier about his employees," the girl hissed hatefully.

"Ohmygod! Blaire, are you okay?" Bethy's voice came from behind me snapping me out of my shock.

I managed to shake off the snails still clinging to my clothing.

"Move," commanded a deep voice that I instantly recognized. My head shot up to find Rush pushing past the couple with the red head who seemed to be laughing at the mess I was in. He was angry. There was no mistaking that. Rush grabbed me by the waist and studied my face a moment. I wasn't sure what for. "Are you okay?" he asked quietly.

I nodded, not sure how to react just yet.

The veins in his neck were once again straining against his skin as he swallowed hard. He barely turned his head to cut his eyes toward the red head. "Don't come near me or her again. Understood?" he said in a deadly calm.

The girl's eyes went wide. "What are you mad at me for? She's the clumsy one. She dumped the whole tray all over herself."

Rush's hands clenched tightly on my hips. "If you utter one more word I'll threaten to remove all my contributions from this club until you are escorted out. Permanently."

The girl gasped, "But I'm Nan's friend, Rush. Her oldest friend. You wouldn't do that to me. Especially for the hired help." The childish pout in her voice was odd coming from a twenty- one year old woman.

"Test me," he replied.

He looked back down at me. "You're coming with me."

I didn't have time to respond before he turned his head to look over my shoulder. "I have her Bethy. She's okay. Go on back to Jace." Rush slipped his hand around my waist. "Watch out for the snails; they're slippery."

Two of the busboys were hurrying into the room with supplies to clean up the mess. The music hadn't stopped but the place had gone quiet. Slowly, people started to talk again. I kept my eyes on the door waiting until I could get outside of this ballroom and break away from Rush's arms.

If everyone in there hadn't known we were having sex, they did now. He'd just shown everyone that he cared about me to an extent, but he didn't exactly want to walk around with me on his arm. My chest ached. I needed my distance from him. It was time I learned to crawl back into my own little world where I trusted me and me only. No one else. Once we were out of the ballroom and away from prying eyes, I stepped free of Rush and put some distance between us. I crossed my arms over my chest and stared down at my feet. I wasn't sure if looking at him was such a good thing yet. I hadn't taken time to enjoy how gorgeous he looked in a black tux. I'd been doing my best not to look at him. Now that he stood right here in front of me dressed like he was while I was in my server dress covered in snail oil, the massive difference between our worlds was evident.

"Blaire, I'm sorry. I wasn't expecting something like that to happen. I didn't even know she had issues with you. I'm going to talk to Nan about this. I have a feeling she had something to do with it—"

"The redhead hates me because of Woods' interest in me. Nan had nothing to do with it and neither did you."

Rush didn't respond right away. I wondered if I should just turn and walk back to the kitchen.

"Is Woods still hitting on you?"

Had he really just asked me that? I was standing there covered in snails and butter and he was asking me if some other guy was hitting on me? I didn't even know if I still had a job. That was it. I'd had enough. I spun around and started for the kitchen. Rush didn't let me get far. His hand shot out and grabbed my arm.

"Blaire, wait. I'm sorry. I shouldn't have asked that. That isn't the issue right now. I wanted to make sure you were okay and help get you cleaned up." His voice was pained as he said the last part.

I sighed and turned back around and met his gaze this time. "I'm fine. I need to go to the kitchen and see if I even still have a job. I was warned by Woods this morning that something like this might happen and it would be my fault. So, right now I have bigger problems than you suddenly feeling the need to be possessive of me. Which is ridiculous. Because you were doing your best to ignore me until this incident happened. You either know me or you don't, Rush. Pick a team." The hurt in my voice hadn't been easy to mask. I jerked my arm free of his hand and stalked back toward the kitchen.

"You were working. What did you want me to do?" he called out and I stopped. "Acknowledging you would have given Nan reason to attack you. I was protecting you."

The fact he even admitted that told me so much. Nan came first. He was ignoring me to keep Nan happy. I'd expected this of course. I was just the booty call. Nan was the sister. He was right to choose her over me. How could he look at me as anything more when I'd gone so easily to his bed?

"You're right, Rush. You ignoring me would keep Nan from attacking me. I'm just the girl you fucked the past two nights. All things considered I'm not that special. I'm one of many." I didn't wait for him to say anymore. I ran for the kitchen doors slamming into them before the tears welling up in my eyes broke free.

TWENTY-TWO

"Whoa, girl," Jimmy said, holding his arms out to catch me as I came barreling into the kitchen.

A hiccup escaped and I swallowed back the sob that followed it.

"That was brutal in there but it could have been worse. At least Rush came to the rescue." Jimmy patted my back and hugged me.

I didn't want Jimmy to know how incredibly cheap I was. I couldn't tell him these tears were because I'd become a rich guys dirty little secret. Not because some mean bitch had dumped food all over me in front of a room full of people.

"Get back out there Jim. We need more servers on the floor. I'll talk to Blaire," Woods said as he walked into the kitchen.

Jimmy hugged me hard one more time then frowned over at

Woods before taking his tray and heading for the door. "You be nice to my girl," Jimmy said as he passed Woods.

Woods didn't reply. Instead he studied me. I figured this was it. The big "it's your fault so you can leave now" moment.

"I go to the trouble of warning you about Nan and it isn't even Rush's fault a jealous bitch attacked you," Woods growled and shook his head in disgust. "I'm sorry, Blaire. This one is all on me. I wasn't expecting that from her. She's the crazy exgirlfriend I can't seem to shake."

He wasn't firing me? I leaned back on the counter behind me to take a deep breath.

"Due to the drama, I don't want you back out there. You can stay in here and help prepare trays though. I'll make sure you make the same amount as you would have made out there."

"Thank you. But can I change?" I asked, needing to get the snail off of me.

Woods smiled, "Yeah. Go get one of the cart girl outfits from the office. We have all our extra server uniforms in use tonight."

I pushed off from the counter and headed for the door.

"Take your time. We are fine in here if you need a break," Woods called out as I exited the kitchen.

Rush and Nan stood in the hallway in what looked like a heated argument when I walked out. Nan shot her icy glare my way. I could see the frustration in Rush's expression. I was only causing him grief. I didn't care to see this. They could have their family quarrel and get over it. After tonight, I should have enough money to move out. Tomorrow I would find a place because sleeping under Rush's roof was going to be impossible. I turned and opened the door leading outside.

"Blaire, wait," Rush called out.

"Let her go, Rush," Nan demanded.

"I can't," he replied.

The door closed behind me and I tried to block out what I'd heard. I didn't need to think or even consider that Rush would fight for me.

The door swung open and Rush came running out of it. "Blaire, please wait. Talk to me," he begged.

I stopped and watched as he ran over to stand in front of me. I had nothing to say to him. I'd said it all.

"I'm sorry. But you're wrong; I didn't ignore you in there. Go ask anyone. My eyes never left you. If there was any question in anyone's mind how I felt about you, the fact I couldn't look away from you while you walked around that room should have answered it." He paused and ran his hand over his hair, and muttered a curse. "Then I saw the look on your face when you saw Bethy with Jace. Something inside me was ripped open. I didn't know what you were thinking but I knew you were realizing the wrongness of tonight. You should have never been there serving everyone. You should have been by my side. I wanted you beside me. I was strung so damn tight waiting on anyone to make a wrong move toward you that I forgot to breathe most of the time."

Rush reached out and ran a finger over my clenched fist. "If you can forgive me, I promise this will never happen again. I love Nan. But I'm done trying to please her. She's my sister and she has some issues she needs to work out. I've told her that I'm going to talk to you about everything. There are some things you need to know." He closed his eyes and took a deep breath. "I'm dealing with the fact that you may walk away from me once you know them and never look back. It scares the hell out of me. I don't know what this is that is going on between us but, from the moment I laid eyes on you, I knew you were going to change my world. I was terrified. The more I watched you, the more you drew me in. I couldn't get close enough."

He was ready to open up to me and let me in. He wasn't just using me. I wasn't just another girl he screwed and tossed aside. He was ready to tell me his secrets. He wanted to keep me. My heart gave up. I'd held back and I'd fought hard to keep him from taking it over. Still, he'd managed to own it. Seeing him vulnerable was the last straw. I couldn't hold back anymore.

I had fallen too far. I was in love with Rush Finlay.

"Okay," I said. There was nothing more to say. He had me.

Rush frowned. "Okay?"

I nodded. "Okay. If you actually want to keep me so badly that you're willing to open up to me, then okay." I would not tell him I loved him. It was too soon. He'd think it was because I was so young. That was something I'd hold close to my chest until I knew it was time. Maybe it was because I was so young. I felt it just the same.

A small grin tugged on his lips. "I just bared my soul to you and all I get is an 'okay'?" he asked.

I shrugged, "You said everything I needed to hear. I'm hooked now. You have me. What are you going to do with me?"

Rush let out a low sexy laugh and pulled me close to him. "I'm thinking sex on the sixteenth hole by the lake would be nice."

I tilted my head as if I were thinking about it. "Hmmm . . . problem is I'm supposed to change and go work in the kitchen the rest of the night."

Rush let out a heavy sigh. "Shit."

I pressed a kiss to his jawline. "You have a sister to escort," I reminded him.

Rush's arms tightened around me. "All I can think about is being inside you. Having you pressed close to me and hearing you make those sexy ass little moans."

Oh. My. My heart rate picked up at the thought.

"If I could walk away from you easily I'd take you into that office and press you up against the wall and bury myself deep inside. But I can't have a quickie with you. You're too damn addictive."

His description had me breathing hard and clinging to his shoulders. "Go change. I'll stand out here so I'm not tempted. Then I'll walk you back to the kitchen," Rush said as he slowly released me.

I needed a moment to get myself under control before I let go of his arms. Then I turned and hurried into the office.

* * *

I didn't see Rush again after he left me at the kitchen door with a quick kiss. The night had been endless and I was exhausted. Preparing food was harder than it looked. After the place had emptied and cleared out we had then been left with the task of cleaning up.

Three hours later it was almost four in the morning. I all but stumbled out into the early morning darkness and headed for my truck. Part of me expected Rush to be waiting, but then he'd have had to sleep in his car so that would have been ridiculous.

I cranked up my truck and headed for his house. I didn't have to work today so I could sleep. I also wouldn't need to find that apartment any longer. As soon as I pulled into the driveway I looked up to see the lights were still on in Rush's room. The top of the house was all lit up compared to the darkness in the rest of it.

The front door was unlocked so I went inside and quietly closed the door behind me. I wondered if Rush was still awake or if he'd just fallen asleep with the lights on? Did I go to my room or his?

I headed up the stairs and found Rush sitting on the floor leaning against his door looking directly at me. What was he doing?

When his eyes met mine he stood up and stalked toward me. I met him half way. He seemed desperate. I just couldn't figure out why. "I need you upstairs. Now," he said in a tight frantic voice.

My heart sped up. Was someone hurt? Was he okay?

I hurried behind him. He closed the door and locked it. He never locked it. Then his hands were on me before we'd even made it up the stairs.

It was as if some wild man had taken over. Rush ran his hands down my hips and over my behind then back up. He grabbed my shirt and ripped it off. I heard a button pop and winced. That was a uniform shirt. I started to ask him what was wrong but his mouth covered mine and his tongue was inside. His hands found the snap on my shorts and jerking them open he began to push them down. The hungry little growls he was making were causing my body to react. I felt the wetness between my legs and the anxious throb start up.

Rush pushed me back on the stairs and jerked off my shoes and pulled my shorts and panties off then grabbed both my knees and pushed them apart. I didn't have time to process before his mouth was on me licking the folds and slipping inside of me. My still tender flesh from the wild sex we'd had last night was extremely sensitive to each caress of his tongue. I began crying out his name. Falling back on my elbows I watched as he rained kisses along my thighs and then buried his face between my legs again to send me panting and begging for more.

"Mine. This is mine," he chanted like a man possessed as he pulled back to look down at me. He ran his fingers through the middle gently and then cut his eyes up at me, "Mine. This sweet pussy is mine, Blaire."

I was ready to agree to anything if he'd make me come. I wanted him inside me first though.

"Tell me it's mine," he demanded.

I nodded and he slipped a finger up inside causing another moan to escape me. "Tell me it is mine," he repeated.

"It's yours, now please Rush, fuck me."

His eyes went wide and he stood up and pushed down the pajama bottoms he was wearing. His erection stood out proudly.

"No condom tonight. I'll pull out. I just need to feel all of you," he said, as he pushed my knees up and lowered himself down until he was at my entrance. He didn't slam into me like I expected. He eased in slow.

"Does it hurt?" he asked as he held himself over me.

It did a little but I wasn't going to admit to that. I wanted him without control. "It feels good," I assured him.

He bit his bottom lip and eased slowly back out. "These stairs are too hard for you. Come here." He bent down and scooped me up in his arms and started up the steps. I'd never been carried by a guy before and I have to say this was an excellent experience. Rush's naked chest holding me was incredible.

"Will you do something for me?" he asked, bending his head down to press small kisses to my nose and eyelids.

"Yes," I replied.

He stopped by the bed and slowly put me down until my feet touched the floor. "Bend over and lay your chest flat on the bed. Put your hands over your head and leave your ass stuck up in the air."

Um . . . okay. I didn't ask why because I had figured that much out. Keeping my feet on the floor, I bent forward and laid on the bed like he asked.

His hand ran over my bottom and he made a pleased sound in his throat. "You have the most perfect ass I've ever seen," he said in a worshipful tone.

Both of his hands found my hips and slowly he entered me pulling me back onto him as he slid inside. He was deeper this way. "Rush!" I cried out as the slight pain hit from the depth he'd reached.

"Fuck, I'm deep," he groaned.

Then he pulled out slowly and his hips began that familiar rocking. I grabbed onto the sheets as my body began to climb toward its climax. It knew what was coming and my legs started to tremble from the pleasure starting to build inside me.

One of Rush's hands slipped down until it was touching my swollen clit and he began rubbing his thumb over it. "God, you're soaking wet," he panted.

My legs stiffened as the orgasm washed over me and then I began to buck, unable to deal with the sensation of Rush still rubbing me. It was so much pleasure that it hurt. Before I could beg for mercy, his hands grabbed my waist and he pulled out of me quickly.

"GAAAAH!" he yelled as I collapsed onto the bed knowing without looking that he'd pulled out before he came.

"Damn baby, if you only knew how fucking incredible your ass looks right now," he said in a breathless voice.

I turned my head to the side unable to lift it and looked at him. "Why?"

A low chuckle rumbled from his chest. "Let's just say I need to clean you up."

Realization dawned on me and the warmth on my bottom that I hadn't noticed before suddenly caught my attention. A giggle broke free and I buried my face in my hands.

I laid there listening as he ran the water and then walked back out to me. The warmth of the washcloth as he wiped me clean of his cum was nice and I slowly started to fall asleep. I was exhausted. I wondered if I'd ever wake up.

TWENTY-THREE

I was alone. I covered my eyes against the morning sun and looked around the room. Rush wasn't up here. That was surprising. I sat up and looked at the clock. It was after ten. No wonder he wasn't up here. I'd slept the morning away. Today we would talk. He was going to let me in. Last night we'd had amazing sex. I needed words now.

I stood up and found my discarded shorts lying on the end of the bed. Rush must have brought them upstairs because I remembered leaving them on the stairs last night. I slipped them on and then looked around for my shirt. One of Rush's tee shirts was folded neatly beside my shorts so I slipped it on and headed downstairs. I was ready to see Rush.

The doors on the family side of the hall were open. I froze. What did that mean? They were always closed. Then I heard voices. I walked toward the second flight of stairs and listened.

My father's familiar voice carried up the stairs from the living room. He was home.

I took the first step and stopped. Could I face him? Would he ask me to leave? Would he know I'd slept with Rush? Would Nan have her mother hate me too? I hadn't had time to work through all of this yet.

My father said my name and I knew I needed to go down there and face this. Whatever it might be. I forced myself down each step. I made it across the foyer and stopped once I could hear them clearly. I needed to know what I was walking into.

"I can't believe you, Rush. What were you thinking? You know who she is? What she means to this family?" It was his mother talking. I'd never met her but I knew.

"You can't hold her responsible. She wasn't even born yet. You have no idea what she's been through. What HE has put her through." Rush was angry.

I started to walk to the door but paused. Wait. What I meant to this family? What was she talking about?

"Don't go getting all high and mighty. You were the one who went and found him for me. So whatever he put her through," she spat, "you started it all. Then you go and *sleep* with her? Really Rush. My God, what were you thinking? You're just like your father."

I reached out to grab the doorframe for support. I didn't know what was coming but my breathing was becoming shallow. I could feel panic rising in my chest.

"Remember who owns this house, mother," Rush's warning was clear.

His mother let out a loud cackle. "Can you believe this? He is turning on me over a girl he just met. Abe, you have to do something."

There was silence. Then my father cleared his throat. "It's his house, Georgie. I can't force him to do anything. I should have expected this. She's so much like her mother."

"What is that supposed to mean?" the woman roared.

My father sighed, "We've been over this before. The reason I left you for her was because she had this draw to her. I couldn't seem to let her go—"

"I KNOW that. I don't want to hear it again. You wanted her so damn badly you left me pregnant with a bunch of wedding invitations to rescind."

"Sweetheart, calm down. I love you. I was just explaining that Blaire has her mother's charisma. It's impossible not to be drawn to her. And she's just as blind to it as her mother was. She can't help it."

"ARGH! Will that woman never leave me alone? Will she always ruin my life? She's gone for crying out loud. I have the man I love back and our daughter finally has her father and now this. *You* go and sleep with this, this girl!"

My body was numb. I couldn't move. I couldn't take deep breaths. I was still dreaming. That was it. I hadn't woken up yet. I closed my eyes tightly forcing myself to wake up from this sick and twisted dream.

"One more word against her and I will have you leave." Rush's tone was cold and hard.

"Georgie, honey, please calm down. Blaire is a good girl. Her being here isn't the end of the world. She needs somewhere to stay. I explained this to you already. I know you hate Rebecca but she was your best friend. The two of you had been friends since you were kids. Until I came along and ruined everything the two of you were like sisters. This is her daughter. Have some compassion."

No. NO. No. No. No. I did not just hear that. This is not real. My mother would never have broken up someone's wedding. She would have never had my dad leave a woman who was pregnant with his child. My mother was a sweet compassionate woman. She would never, ever let that happen. I couldn't stand here and listen to them talk about her that way. They had it all wrong. They didn't know her. My father had been gone so long he'd forgotten what really happened.

I let go of the death grip I had on the door frame and stalked into the room where they were disgracing my mother's name. "NO! Shut up all of you," I yelled. The room went silent. I found my father and leveled my angry glare on him. No one else in here mattered right now. Not the woman who continued to spit lies about my mother or the man I thought I loved. The one I'd given my body to. The one who had been lying to me.

"Blaire," Rush's voice sounded far away. I held out my hand to stop him. I didn't want him near me.

"You," I pointed my finger at my father. "You are just letting them lie about my mother," I screamed. I didn't care if I looked crazy. I hated them all right now.

"Blaire, let me explain—"

"SHUT UP!" I roared. "My sister, my other half, died. She died, Dad. In a car on her way to the store with YOU. It was like my soul had been taken from me and torn in two. Losing her was unbearable. I watched my mother wail and cry and mourn and then I watched my father walk away. Never to return. While his daughter and wife were trying to pick up the pieces of their world without Valerie in it. Then my mother gets sick. I call you but you don't answer. So, I get an extra job after school and I start making payments for mom's medical care. I do nothing but care for my mother and go to school. Except my senior year, she gets so sick that I have to drop out. Take my GED and be done with it. Because I had the only person on the planet who loved me dying as I sat and watched helplessly. I held her hand while she took her last breath. I arranged her funeral. I watched them lower her into the ground. You never once called. Not once. Then I had to sell the house Gran left us and everything of value in it just to pay off medical bills." I stopped and took a loud heaving breath and a sob escaped me.

Two arms wrapped around me and I screamed, slinging my arms and moving away. "DON'T TOUCH ME!" I didn't want him touching me. He had lied to me. He knew this and he hadn't said a word.

"Now I'm being forced to hear you talk about my mother who was a saint. Do you hear me? She was a saint! You are all *liars*. If anyone is guilty of this bullshit I hear pouring out of your mouth it is that man." I pointed at my father. I couldn't call him that anymore. Not now.

"He is the liar. He isn't worth the dirt beneath my feet. If Nan is his daughter. If you were pregnant." I swung my eyes to the woman I had yet to look at and the words froze on my lips. I remembered her. I staggered back and shook my head. No. This was not what it looked like.

"Who are you?" I asked, as the memories of that face slowly came back to me.

"Careful how you answer that," Rush's tight voice came from behind me. He was still close to me.

Her eyes shifted from me to my father then back to me. "You know who I am Blaire. We've met before."

"You came to my house. You . . . you made my mother cry."

The woman rolled her eyes.

"Last warning, mother," Rush said.

"Nan wanted to meet her father. So I brought her to him. She got to see his nice little family with pretty, blonde twin daughters he loved and an equally perfect wife. I was tired of having to tell my daughter she didn't have a father. She knew she did. So I showed her just what he had chosen instead of her. She didn't ask about him again until much later in life."

The little girl my age that had stood holding her mother's

hand tightly and studying me as I stood at the door. It had been Nan. My stomach rolled. What had my father done?

"Blaire, please look at me." Rush's desperate voice came from behind me but I couldn't acknowledge him. He knew all this. This had been Nan's big secret. He had protected it for her. Did he not see this was my secret too? He was my father and I knew nothing. Woods' words rang in my head. "If he has to choose between you and Nan he will choose Nan."

He knew then that Rush had chosen Nan. Everyone in this town knew the secret but me. They all knew who I was but I didn't.

"I was engaged to Georgianna. She was pregnant with Nan. Your mother came to visit her. She was like no one I'd ever met. She was addictive. I couldn't seem to stay away from her. Georgianna was still pinning over Dean and Rush was still visiting his dad every other weekend. I expected Georgie to go to Dean the minute he decided he wanted a family. I wasn't even sure Nan was mine. Your mother was innocent and fun. She wasn't into rockers and she made me laugh. I pursued her and she ignored me. Then I lied to her. I told her Georgie was pregnant with another of Dean's kids. She felt sorry for me. I somehow convinced her to run away with me. To throw away the friendship she'd had all her life."

I pressed my hands over my ears to block out my dad's words. I couldn't listen to this. It was all lies. This sick world they lived in wasn't for me. I wanted to go home. Back to Alabama. Back to what I understood. Where money and rock stars weren't an issue.

"Stop. I don't want to hear it. I just want my things. I just want to leave." The sob that followed couldn't be helped. My world had just been blown to a million pieces. I needed to go sit by my mother's grave and talk to her. I wanted to go home.

"Baby, please talk to me. Please." Rush was behind me again. I was too tired to push him away. I moved away from him instead. I would not look at him. "I can't look at you. I don't want to talk to you. I just want my things. I want to go home."

"Blaire, honey, there is no home." My dad's voice grated on my nerves. I lifted my eyes and glared at him. All the pain and bitterness I'd kept from creeping in when he left us had consumed me.

"My mother and my sister's graves are home. I want to be near them. I've stood here and listened to y'all tell me my mother was someone who I know she wasn't. She would have never done what you're accusing her of. Stay here with your family, Abe. I'm sure they will love you as much as your last one did. Try not to kill any of them," I spat.

Georgianna's loud gasp was the last thing I heard before I left the room. I wanted to leave but I needed my purse and my keys. I ran up the stairs and threw everything I could back into my luggage and slammed it shut. I swung my purse strap over my shoulder and turned to the door to see Rush standing there watching me.

His face was pale and his eyes were blood shot. I closed my

eyes. I did not care that he was upset. He should be. He'd lied to me. He'd betrayed me.

"You can't leave me," he said in a hoarse whisper.

"Watch me," I replied in a cold flat voice.

"Blaire, you didn't let me explain. I was going to tell you everything today. They came home last night and I panicked. I needed to tell you first." He slammed his fist against the door frame. "You were not supposed to find out that way. Not like that. God *not like that*." He sounded truly upset.

I couldn't let the tugging at my heart from the look on his face get to me. I would be an idiot if I did. Besides, Nan was his sister. No wonder he'd grown up protecting her. She'd been the child without a dad. I swallowed the bile in my throat. My dad was a horrible man.

"I can't stay here. I can't see you. You represent the pain and betrayal of not just me but my mom." I shook my head. "Whatever we had is over. It died the minute I walked downstairs and realized the world I'd always known was a lie."

Rush dropped his hands from the doorframe and his shoulders sagged as he hung his head. He didn't say anything. He just stepped back so I could get out. The little heart that I had left in tact shattered from his defeated look. There was no other way. We were tainted.

TWENTY-FOUR

I didn't look back and he didn't call my name again. I headed down the stairs with my suitcase in hand. When I got to the bottom step, my dad came out of the living room and into the foyer. A frown was etched on his face. He looked fifteen years older since the last time I'd seen him. The past five years hadn't been good to him.

"Don't leave, Blaire. Let's talk about this. Give yourself time to think about things." He wanted me to stay. Why? So he could make himself feel better for ruining my life? For ruining Nan's life?

I pulled the phone he'd wanted me to have out of my pocket and held it out to him. "Take it. I don't want it," I said.

He stared down at it and then back at me. "Why would I take your phone?"

"Because I don't want anything from you," I replied. The anger was there but I was tired. I just wanted out of here.

"I didn't give you that phone," he said, still looking confused.

"Take the phone, Blaire. If you want to leave, I can't hold you here. But please, take the phone." Rush was standing at the top of the stairs. He'd bought me the phone. My dad had never told him to get one for me. The numbness was settling in. I couldn't feel any more pain. No sorrow for what we might have had.

I walked over and put the phone down on the table beside the stairs. "I can't," was my simple reply. I didn't look back at any of them. Although I'd heard Georgianna's heels click on the marble floor alerting me that she had entered the foyer.

I grabbed the door handle and pulled the door open. I would never see any of them again. I'd only mourn the loss of one.

"You look just like her." Georgianna's voice rang out in the silent foyer. I knew she meant my mother. She had no right even to remember my mother. Or speak of her. She'd lied about my mother. She'd made the one woman I admired above everyone else seem selfish and cruel.

"I only hope I can be half the woman she was," I said in a loud clear voice. I wanted them all to hear me. They needed to know there was no doubt in my mind that my mother was innocent.

I stepped out into the sunshine and closed the door firmly behind me. A silver sports car spun into the drive as I made my way to my truck. I knew it was Nan. I couldn't look at her. Not now.

The car door slammed and I didn't flinch. I threw my suitcase into the back of the truck and opened the door. I was done here.

"You know," she said in a loud amused tone.

I would not respond to her. I would not listen to her mouth spew more lies about my mother.

"How's it feel? Knowing you were left for someone else by your own father?"

It felt numb. That was the least of my pain. My dad had left us five years ago. I'd moved on.

"You don't feel so high and mighty now, do ya? Your momma was a cheap hussy that deserved what she got."

The calmness that had settled over me snapped. No one was gonna talk about my momma again. No one. I reached under the seat and pulled out my nine millimeter. I turned and aimed at her lying red lips.

"You say one more word about my momma and I'll put an extra hole in your body," I said in a hard flat voice.

Nan screamed and threw her hands up in the air. I didn't lower the gun. I wasn't going to kill her. I'd just wing her in the arm if she opened her mouth again. My aim was spot on.

"Blaire! Put the gun down. Nan, don't move. She knows how to use that thing better than most men." My dad's voice caused my hands to tremble. He was protecting her. From me. His daughter. The one he wanted. The one he left us for. The one he'd deserted most of her life. I didn't know what to feel.

I heard Georgianna's panicked voice. "What is she doing with that thing? Is that even legal for her to have it?"

"She has a permit," my father replied, "and she knows what she's doing. Stay calm."

I lowered the gun. "I'm gonna get in that truck and drive out of your life. Forever. Just keep your mouth shut about my momma. I won't listen to it again," I warned before turning and climbing into my truck. I tucked my gun back under the seat and backed out of the driveway. I didn't look to see if they were all huddled around poor Nannette. I didn't care. Maybe she'd think twice before she fucked with someone else's momma. Because, by God, she better never talk bad about mine again.

I headed to the country club. I'd have to tell them I was leaving. Darla deserved to know not to expect me. So did Woods for that matter. I didn't want to explain but they probably already knew. Everyone knew but me. They'd all just been waiting on me to find out. Why one of them couldn't have told me the truth I didn't understand.

It wasn't like this was life altering for Nan. Everything she'd ever known hadn't just been blown to hell. My life had just flipped on its axis. This wasn't about Nan. This was about me. Me, dammit. Why did they have to protect her? What did she need protecting from?

I parked the truck outside the office and Darla met me at the front door.

"You forget to check the schedule, girl? This is your day off." She was smiling at me but it vanished when my eyes met hers. She stopped walking and grabbed the railing on the porch of the office. Then she shook her head. "You know, don't you?"

Even Mrs. Darla had known. I simply nodded. She let out a long-winded sigh, "I'd heard the rumors like most folks but no one knew the whole truth. I don't want to know 'cause it ain't my business, but if it's close to what I've heard then I know this hurts." Darla walked down the rest of the stairs. The commanding little firecracker I knew was gone. She opened her arms when she got to the bottom step and I ran into them. I didn't think about it. I needed someone to hold me. The sobs came the moment she wrapped me up in her arms.

"I know it sucks, sugar. I wish someone would've told you sooner."

I couldn't talk. I just cried and clung to her while she held on tight.

"Blaire? What's wrong?" Bethy's voice sounded worried and I looked up to see her running down the steps toward us. "Oh shit. You know," she said, stopping in her tracks. "I should've told you but I was scared to. I didn't know all the facts. I just knew what Jace had overheard from Nan. I didn't want to tell you the wrong thing. I was hoping Rush would tell you. He did, didn't he? I thought for sure he would after the way I saw him looking at you last night."

I eased back out of Darla's arms and wiped at my face. "No. He didn't tell me. I overheard. My dad and Georgianna came home."

"Shit," Bethy said in a frustrated sigh. "Are you leaving?" The pained expression in her eyes told me she already knew the answer to that.

I only nodded.

"Where will you go?" Darla asked.

"Back to Alabama. Back home. I have some money saved up now. I'll be able to find a job and I do have friends there. My mom and sister's graves are there." I didn't finish. I couldn't without breaking down again.

"We'll miss you around here," Darla said with a sad smile.

I would miss them too. All of them. Even Woods. I nodded. "Me too."

Bethy let out a loud sob and running over to me she threw her arms around my neck. "I never had a friend like you before. I don't want you to leave."

My eyes filled up with tears again. I'd made a few friend here. Not everyone had betrayed me. "Maybe you could come to Bama and visit sometime," I whispered in a choked sob.

She pulled back and sniffed. "You'd let me come visit?"

"Of course," I replied.

"Okay. Is next week too soon?"

If I could've managed the energy to smile, I would have. I doubted I'd ever smile again. "As soon as you're ready."

She nodded and rubbed her red nose with her arm.

"I'll let Woods know. He'll understand," Darla said from behind us.

"Thank you."

"You be careful. Take care. Let us know how you're doing."

"I will," I replied, wondering if it would be a lie. Would I ever talk to them again?

Darla stepped back and motioned for Bethy to come stand beside her. I waved at them both and opened the truck door to climb in. It was time I left this place behind.

TWENTY-FIVE

The sigh of relief I expected when I drove under the first out of only three traffic lights in Sumit, Alabama, didn't come. The numbness had taken over completely on my seven-hour drive. The words I'd heard my father say about my mother replayed over and over in my head until I couldn't feel anything for anyone.

I turned left at traffic light number two and headed for the cemetery. I needed to talk to momma before I checked into the only motel in town. I wanted to let her know that I didn't believe any of it. I knew what kind of woman she was. What kind of mother she was. No one would ever compare. She'd been my rock when she'd been the one dying. Never had I feared that she'd walk away from me.

The gravel parking lot was empty. The last time I'd been here most of the town had come to pay their last respects to my mom. Today the afternoon sun was fading away and the shadows were the only company I had.

Stepping out of my truck, I swallowed the lump that had risen in my throat. Being here again. Knowing she was here but she wasn't. I walked down the path to her grave wondering if anyone had come to see her while I'd been gone. She had friends. Surely someone had stopped by with fresh flowers. My eyes stung. I didn't like thinking she'd been left alone for weeks. I was glad that I'd had them bury her beside Valerie. It had made the walking away easier.

The fresh patch of dirt was now covered in grass. Mr. Murphy had told me he would cover it in sod for free. I hadn't been able to pay any extra. Seeing the green grass made me feel like she was properly covered as silly as that sounded. Her grave looked just like Valerie's now. The headstone wasn't as fancy as my sister's. It was a simple; it had been all I could afford. I'd spent hours trying to decide exactly what I wanted it to say.

Rebecca Hanson Wynn

April 19, 1967 – June 2, 2012

The love she left behind will be the reason dreams are reached. She was the rock in a world that was crumbling. Her strength will remain. It's in our hearts.

The family that loved me was no longer here. Standing here looking at their graves it rang home how alone I really was. I didn't have family anymore. I would never acknowledge my father's existence after this day.

"I didn't expect you back so soon." I'd heard the gravel crunch behind me and I'd known without turning around who it was. I didn't look at him. I wasn't ready yet. He'd see through me. Cain had been my friend since kindergarten. The year we'd become something more it was just expected. I'd loved him for years.

"My life is here," I replied simply.

"I tried to argue that point a few weeks ago." The touch of humor in his voice didn't go unnoticed. He liked being right. He always had.

"I thought I needed my father's help. I didn't."

The gravel crunched a little more as he stepped up beside me. "He still an ass?"

I only nodded. I wasn't ready to tell Cain just what an ass my father was. I couldn't voice that right now. Saying it out loud made it real somehow. I wanted to believe it was a dream.

"You not like his new family?" Cain asked. He wouldn't let up. He would ask me questions until I broke down and told him everything.

"How did you know I was home?" I asked, changing the subject. It would only sidetrack him for a moment but I didn't intend to stand around long.

"You didn't really expect to drive your truck through town and it not become the number one source of headline news within five minutes? You know this place better than that, B."

B. He'd called me B since we were five. He had called Valerie, Ree. Nicknames. Memories. It was safe. This town was safe.

"Have I even been here five minutes?" I asked still studying the grave in front of me. My mother's name etched in stone.

"Naw, probably not. I was sitting outside the grocery store waiting on Callie to get off work," he trailed off. He was seeing Callie again. Not surprising. She seemed to be the one he couldn't get out of his system.

I took a deep breath then finally turned my head and looked into his blue eyes. Emotion battled past the numbness I was hugging close to me like a cloak. This was home. This was safe. This was all what I knew.

"I'm staying," I told him.

A grin tugged at his lips and he nodded. "I'm glad. You've been missed. This is where you belong, B."

A few weeks ago I'd thought with momma gone I didn't fit in anywhere. Maybe I had been wrong. My past was here.

"I don't want to talk about Abe," I told him and shifted my gaze back to my mother's grave.

"Done. I'll never bring him up again."

I didn't have to say anything else. I closed my eyes and prayed silently that my mom and sister were together and happy. Cain didn't move. We stood there without speaking as the sun set.

When the darkness had finally settled over the cemetery, Cain slipped his hand into mine. "Come on, B. Let's go find you somewhere to stay."

I let him lead me back down the path and to my truck. "Will you let me take you to Granny's? She has a guest bedroom and she'd love to have you stay there. She's all alone in that house. She might even call me less if she has some company."

Granny Q was Cain's mother's mother. She'd been my Sunday school teacher all during elementary school. She had also sent us meals once a week when my mom got too sick.

"I have some money. I was going to get a motel. I don't want to impose on her."

Cain let out a hard laugh, "If she finds out you're in a hotel room she'll show up at the door raising hell. You'll be in her house when she's done with you. It's easier just to go to her house now instead of causing a scene. Besides, B, there is one motel in this town. You and I both know how many date nights have ended up at that place. Major yuck factor."

He was right.

"You don't have to take me. I'll go see her myself. You have Callie waiting on you," I reminded him.

He rolled his eyes. "Don't go there, B. You know better. Snap of your fingers, babe. Just a snap of your fingers. That's all it would take."

He'd been telling me that for years. It was a joke now. At least to me it was. My heart wasn't there. Silver eyes flashed in my mind and the pain broke through the numbness. I knew where my heart was and I wasn't sure I'd ever see it again. Not if I was going to survive.

Granny Q wouldn't let me sit quietly. She wouldn't let me settle. Tonight I needed peace. Solitude.

"Cain. I need this night alone. I need to think. I need to

process. Tonight I need to stay at the motel. Please understand and help Granny understand. Just for tonight."

Cain looked out over my head with a frustrated scowl. I knew he wanted to ask questions but he was being careful. "B, I hate this. I know you're hurting. I can see it all over your face. I've watched you hurt for so many years. It is slowly eating me up. Talk to me, B. You need to talk to someone."

He was right. I did need to talk to someone but right now I needed to worry about dealing internally. I'd tell him about Rosemary Beach eventually. I'd have to tell someone. Cain was the closest friend I had here.

"Give me some time," I said, looking up at him.

"Time," he nodded. "I've been giving you time for three years. I don't see how a little more can hurt."

I opened the truck door and climbed inside. Tomorrow I'd be ready to face the truth. The facts. I could make it . . . tomorrow.

"Do you have a phone? I called your old number the day after you drove off and left me here and it said it was disconnected."

Rush. His face when he'd begged me to keep the phone he'd lied about flashed in my mind. The pain pressed through a little more.

I shook my head. "No. I don't have one."

Cain's scowl deepened. "Dangit, B. You shouldn't be without a phone."

"I got a gun," I reminded him.

"You still need a phone. I doubt you've ever pulled that thing out on anyone in your life."

That was where he was wrong. I shrugged.

"Get one tomorrow," he ordered. I nodded although I didn't intend to get one then closed the truck door behind me.

I pulled back out onto the two-lane street. I drove the half mile up to the first traffic light and turned right. The motel was the second building on the left. I had never stayed here before. I had friends who had come here after prom but that was all a part of high school I only heard about in the hallways.

Paying for the night was easy enough. The girl working the desk looked familiar but she was younger than me. Probably still in high school. I got my key and headed back outside.

The shiny black Range Rover that was parked beside my truck looked so out of place here. The heart I'd thought was numb slammed hard against my chest in one painful thud as my eyes connected with Rush's. He was standing in front of the Range Rover with his hands in his pockets watching me.

I didn't expect to see him again. At least not this soon. I'd made it clear how I felt. How had he known how to get here? I'd never told him the name of my hometown. Had my father? Did they not understand I wanted to be left alone?

A car door slammed and my attention was jerked off Rush to see Cain stepping out of the red Ford truck he'd gotten for graduation. "I'm hoping like hell you know this guy 'cause he's followed you here from the cemetery. I noticed him on the side of the road watching us a ways back but I didn't say anything," Cain said, as he sauntered over to stand slightly in front of me.

"I know him," I managed to get past the tightness in my throat.

Cain glanced back at me, "He the reason you came running home?"

No. Not really. He wasn't what sent me running. He was what had made me want to stay. Even knowing everything we might have had was impossible.

"No," I said, shaking my head and looking back at Rush. Even in the moonlight his face looked pained.

"Why are you here?" I asked, keeping my distance. Cain shifted more in front of me when he realized I wasn't going near Rush.

"You're here," he replied.

God. How was I going to get through this again? Seeing him and knowing I couldn't have him. What he represented would always dirty anything that I felt for him.

"I can't do this, Rush."

He took a step forward, "Talk to me. Please, Blaire. There is so much I need to explain."

I shook my head and took a step backward. "No. I can't."

Rush cursed and shifted his gaze from me to Cain. "Could you give us a minute?" he demanded.

Cain crossed his arms over his chest and took one more step to stand in front of me. "I don't think so. It doesn't seem like she wants to talk to you. Can't say I'm gonna make her. And neither are you."

I didn't have to see Rush to know Cain had just majorly pissed him off. If I didn't stop them this would end badly. I stepped around Cain and walked toward Rush and the direction of my room. If we were going to talk we weren't going to have an audience.

"It's okay, Cain. This is my stepbrother, Rush Finlay. He already knows who you are. He wants to talk. So we are going to talk. You can leave. I'll be fine," I said over my shoulder and then turned to unlock room 4A.

"Stepbrother? Wait . . . Rush Finlay? As in Dean Finlay's only child? Shit B, you're related to a rock celebrity."

I'd forgotten what a fan Cain was of rock bands. He would know all about the only son of Slacker Demon's drummer.

"Go, Cain," I repeated. I opened my door and stepped inside.

TWENTY-SIX

I put the entire length of the room between us. I didn't stop until I was standing against the wall on the other side of the room.

Rush followed me inside and closed the door behind him. His eyes looked like they were drinking me in.

"Talk. Hurry. I want you gone," I told him.

Rush flinched from my words. I would not allow myself to feel for him. I couldn't.

"I love you."

No. He was not saying that. I shook my head. No. I was not hearing this. He did not love me. He couldn't. Love didn't lie.

"I know my actions don't appear to back that up but if you'd just let me explain. God, baby, I can't stand seeing you in so much pain."

He had no idea the extent of the pain. He had known how much I loved my mother. How important she was to me. How much she had sacrificed. He knew it all and he still didn't tell me what they thought of my mother. What *he* thought of my mother. I couldn't love that. Him. Anyone who mocked my mother's memory. I could never love that. Ever.

"Nothing you can say will fix this. She was my mother, Rush. The one memory that holds anything good in my life. She is the center of every happy childhood moment I have. And you . . ." I closed my eyes unable to look at him. "And you, and . . . and them . . . y'all disgraced her. The ugly lies that you spoke as if they were the truth."

"I'm so sorry you found out this way. I wanted to tell you. At first, you were just a product that would hurt Nan. I thought you'd cause her more pain. The problem was that you fascinated me. I'll admit I was immediately drawn to you because you're gorgeous. It was breathtaking. I hated you because of it. I didn't want to be attracted to you. But I was. I wanted you bad that very first night. Just to be near you, God, I made up reasons to find you. Then . . . then I got to know you. I was hypnotized by your laugh. It was the most amazing sound I'd ever heard. You were so honest and determined. You didn't whine or complain. You took what life handed you and worked with it. I wasn't used to that. Every time I watched you, every time I was near you I fell a little more." Rush took a step toward me and I held up both my hands to hold him back. I was taking deep breaths. I would not cry again. If he needed to tell me all this and completely devastate me even more then I would listen. I'd give him his closure because I knew I'd never get mine.

"Then that night at the honky-tonk. You owned me after that. You may not have realized it but I was hooked. There was no going back for me. I had so much to make up for. I'd put you through hell since you'd arrived and I hated myself for it. I wanted to give you the world. But I knew . . . I knew who you were. When I let myself remember exactly who you were I would pull back. How could I be so completely wrapped up in the girl who represented my sister's pain?"

I covered my ears. "No. I won't listen to this. Leave, Rush. Leave now!" I yelled. I didn't want to hear about Nan. Her vile words about my mother rang in my ears and I felt the need to scream bubbling in my chest. Anything to block it out.

"The day mom came home from the hospital with her I was three. I remember it though. She was so small and I remember worrying that something would happen to her. My mom cried a lot. So did Nan. I grew up fast. By the time Nan was three I was doing everything from fixing her breakfast to tucking her in at night. Our mom had married and now we had Grant. There was never any stability. I actually looked forward to the times my dad would come get me because I wouldn't be responsible for Nan for a few days. I'd get a break. Then she began asking why I had a daddy and she didn't."

"Stop!" I warned him, moving further down the wall. Why was he doing this to me?

"Blaire, I need you to hear me. This is the only way you'll understand." His voice was broken. "Mom would tell her she didn't have one because she was special. That didn't work for every long. I went and demanded that mom tell me who Nan's dad was. I wanted it to be mine. I knew my dad would take her places. Mom told me that Nan's dad had another family. He had two little girls he loved more than Nan. He wanted those girls but he didn't want Nan. I couldn't understand how anyone couldn't want Nan. She was my little sister. Sure, at times I wanted to kill her, but I loved her fiercely. Then came the day Mom took her to see the family her father had chosen. She cried for months afterward." He stopped and I sank down on the bed. He was going to make me listen to this. I couldn't get him to stop.

"I hated those girls. I hated that family that Nan's dad had chosen over her. I swore one day I'd make him pay. Nan would always say maybe one day he'd come see her. She daydreamed about him wanting to see her. I listened to these dreams for years. When I was nineteen, I went looking for him. I knew his name. I found him. I left him a picture of Nan with our address on the back. I told him he had another daughter who was special and she just wanted to meet him. To talk to him."

That was five years ago. My stomach twisted. I felt sick. I'd lost Valerie five years ago. He'd left five years ago.

"I did it because I loved my sister. I had no idea what his other family was going through. I didn't care honestly. I only cared about Nan. You were the enemy. Then you walked into my house and completely changed my world. I always swore I'd never feel guilty for breaking up that family. After all, they had broken up Nan's. Every moment I was with you the guilt at what I'd done started to eat me alive. Seeing your eyes when you told me about your sister and your mom. God, I swear you ripped my heart out that night, Blaire. I will never get over that." Rush walked over to me and I was unable to move.

I understood. I did. But in the understanding I'd lost my own heart. It all was a lie. My entire life. It was a lie. All those memories. The Christmases that mom baked cookies and Dad held Valerie and I up so we could decorate the top of the tree were all false. They couldn't be real. I believed Rush. It didn't change how I viewed my mother. She wasn't here to tell her side to the story. I knew enough to know that she was innocent. She couldn't be anything but. This was all my father's sin.

"I swear to you that as much as I love my sister if I could go back and change things I would. I would have NEVER gone to see your dad. Ever. I'm so sorry, Blaire. I'm so fucking sorry." His voice broke and I lifted my eyes to see his eyes wet with unshed tears.

If he hadn't gone to see my dad, things would have been so different. But neither of us could change the past no matter how badly we wanted to. Neither of us could make this right. Nan had her father now. She had what she'd always wanted. So, did Georgianna.

I had me.

"I can't tell you that I forgive you," I said. Because I couldn't. "But I can tell you that I understand why you did what you did. It altered my world. That can never be changed."

A lone tear ran down Rush's face. I couldn't reach up and wipe it away just like the tears were now gone for me. "I don't want to lose you. I'm in love with you Blaire. I've never wanted anything or anyone the way I want you. I can't imagine my world now without you in it."

I would always only have just me. Because this man had taken my heart and destroyed it. Even if he hadn't meant to. I'd never trust enough to love again.

"I can't love you, Rush."

A choked sob rocked his body as he dropped his head in my lap. I didn't console him. I couldn't. How did I soothe his ache when mine was a big gaping hole large enough for both of us to fit in?

"You don't have to love me. Just don't leave me," he said against my leg.

Would my life always be full of loss? I hadn't been able to tell my sister goodbye when she left that day and never returned. I had refused to tell my mother goodbye that morning when she told me it was almost time. She'd closed her eyes and never opened them again. I knew once Rush left this room that it would be the last time I saw him. It would be our final goodbye. I couldn't move on with my life if he was in it. He would always hinder my healing.

But I wanted my goodbye this time. This was my final goodbye and this time I wanted a chance to say it properly. I couldn't say the words. They refused to come. My need to protect my mother's name stood between me and the words I knew Rush needed to hear. I couldn't tell him I forgave him knowing that he was the reason my dad had walked out and never come back. He had taken my dad away that day even if he hadn't known the damage that picture would do.

None of that changed how I had felt for Rush before he'd blown my world into a million pieces. I would get my goodbye.

TWENTY-SEVEN

"Rush."

He lifted his head. His face was wet with tears. I wouldn't wipe them. They served a purpose. I stood up unsnapping my shirt and slipped it off to lay it down on the bed. I then discarded my bra. Rush's eyes never left my body. The confusion on his face was expected. I couldn't explain this. I just needed it.

I pushed down the shorts I was wearing and stepped out of them. Then slipped off my shoes and slowly took off my panties. Once I was completely bare I stepped over to straddle Rush's legs. His hands wrapped around me immediately and he buried his face in my stomach. The wetness from his tears was cold against my skin causing me to shiver.

"What are you doing, Blaire?" Rush asked pulling back just enough to look up at me. I couldn't answer that.

I grabbed handfuls of his shirt and pulled at it until he raised his arms and let me pull it over his head and toss it aside. Sinking down until I was sitting in his lap, I slipped my hands behind his head and kissed him. Slowly. This was the last time. Rush's hands were in my hair and he took over immediately. Each caress of his tongue was gentle and easy. He wasn't hungry and demanding. Maybe he already knew this was goodbye. It wasn't meant to be hard and fast. It was the last memory I'd have of him. Of us. The only one I'd have where a lie didn't dirty the water. The truth was there between us now.

"Are you sure?" Rush whispered against my mouth as I rocked against the hardness that I already felt beneath his jeans.

I only nodded.

Rush picked me up and laid me down on the bed before slipping off his shoes and jeans. He crawled over me as his haunted face studied me. "You're the most beautiful woman I've ever seen. Inside and out," he whispered as he rained kisses on my face before pulling my bottom lip into his mouth and sucking.

I lifted my hips. I needed him inside. I would always need him inside but this would be the last time I had him there. This close. No one would ever be this close again. No one.

Rush ran his hands down my body taking time to touch every part. As if he were memorizing me. I arched into his hands and closed my eyes letting the feel of his hands brand me. "I love you so damn much," he swore as his head lowered to kiss my belly button.

I let my legs fall open so that he could move between them.

"Do I need to wear a condom?" he asked, moving back up over me.

Yes, he did. No chances.

Again, I just nodded.

He stood up to pick up his jeans and pulled a condom out of his wallet. I watched him rip it open then slide it down over his cock. I'd never kissed him there before. I'd thought about it but I'd never had the nerve. Somethings should remain unknown.

Rush ran his hands up the inside of my legs and then slowly pushed them open wider. "This will always be mine," he said with conviction.

I didn't correct him. There was no use. It would never be anyone else's. After today, I would belong only to myself.

Rush lowered his body over mine until I could feel the head of his erection pressing against me. "Never been this good. Nothing has ever been this good," he groaned then slid inside me. The stretch was welcomed. I wrapped my hands around his arms and cried out as he filled me completely.

Slowly, he moved out and then rocked back into me. His eyes never left mine. I held his gaze. I could see the storm in his eyes. I knew he was confused. I could even see the fear. Then there was the love. I saw it. The fierceness in his eyes. I believed it. I could see it clearly. But it was too late now. The love wasn't enough. Everyone always said that love was enough. It wasn't. Not when your soul was shattered.

I slipped my legs up around his waist and then wrapped my arms around his neck. Close. I needed him close. His breath was warm on my neck as he pressed kisses against the tender skin there. He whispered words of love and promises he would never have to keep. I let him. Just this last time.

The pleasure that had been building reached its peak when Rush brushed a kiss against my lips and said, "Only you."

I didn't look away from him as I clung to him and let the feeling of complete bliss rush through me. Rush's mouth opened and a loud growl vibrated his chest as he pumped into me two more times and then went still. His eyes never left mine.

We both breathed fast and hard as I said all that needed to be said without words. It was in my eyes. If he was looking closely enough.

"Don't do this, Blaire," he pleaded.

"Goodbye, Rush."

He shook his head. He was still buried deep inside me. "No. Don't you do this to us."

I didn't say anything more. I let my hands fall to my side and my legs slip down his waist until I was no longer clinging to him. I wouldn't argue with him.

"I didn't get a goodbye with my sister or my mom. Those were final goodbyes I never got. This final goodbye I needed. This one time between us with no lies."

Rush grabbed the blankets underneath me in both hands and closed his eyes tightly. "No. No. Please, don't."

I wanted to reach up and touch his face. To tell him it would be okay. He'd move on and get over this. Us. But I couldn't do that. How could I comfort him if I was empty inside?

Rush pulled out of me and I winced at the hollowness that echoed through my body. He stood up and didn't look at me. I watched in silence as he began to dress himself. This was it. Was empty supposed to hurt? When would the pain stop showing up?

Once he had his shirt back on he lifted his eyes to look at me. I sat up and pulled my knees against my chest to cover my nudity and to hold myself together. I was afraid I might literally crumble.

"I can't make you forgive me. I don't deserve your forgiveness. I can't change the past. All I can do is give you what you want. If this is what you want, I'll walk away, Blaire. It'll kill me but I'll do it."

What else could there be? I'd never be the same. The girl he'd fallen in love with was no more. He'd see that soon enough if he stayed. I didn't have a past. I didn't have a foundation. It was all gone. Nothing made sense and I knew it never would. Rush deserved more.

"Goodbye, Rush," I said one last time.

The pain that clouded his eyes was too much. I dropped my gaze from his and studied the blue plaid blanket beneath me.

I listened as he walked toward the door. His footsteps were muffled on the old faded carpet. Then the door opened and the moonlight poured into the dark room. There was a pause. I wondered if he would say more. I didn't want him to. Every word he said only made this harder.

The door closed. I lifted my eyes to see the empty motel room surrounding me. Goodbyes weren't all they were cracked up to be. I knew that now.

ACKNOWLEDGEMENTS

This book would have never made it to publication without the following people reading it and giving me invaluable advice and encouragement:

Colleen Hoover, Liz Reinhardt, Elizabeth Reyes, Tracey Garves- Graves, Angie Stanton, Tammara Webber, Autumn Hull and Nichole Chase. They all were there when I wasn't sure I should release this one. They didn't let me doubt myself. This book is thanks to them. Love you all ladies.

Sarah Hansen who designed this amazing cover. She is brilliant. I love her and she's pretty dang fun to hang out with too. Trust me . . . I know ;)

Keith, my husband, who tolerated the dirty house, lack of clean clothes, and my mood swings, while I wrote this book (and all my other books).

My three precious kiddos who ate a lot of corn dogs, pizza, and Frosted Flakes because I was locked away writing. I promise, I cooked them many good hot meals once I finished.

To the coolest agent to ever grace the literary world, Jane Dystel. I adore her. It is that simple. And a shout out to Lauren Abramo, my foreign rights agent who is doing an amazing job at getting my books worldwide. She rocks.

Stephanie T. Lott I've worked with many editors and I really love this one. She's fabulous.